PROCESS

A NOVEL BY

KAY BOYLE

process

EDITED AND WITH

AN INTRODUCTION BY

SANDRA SPANIER

UNIVERSITY OF

ILLINOIS PRESS

Urbana and Chicago

© 2001 by the Board of Trustees
of the University of Illinois
Manufactured in the United States of America
C 1 2 3 4 5
∞ This book is printed on acid-free paper.

Frontispiece: Kay Boyle, Cincinnati, 1918.
(Kay Boyle Papers, Morris Library, Southern Illinois
University, Carbondale)

Library of Congress Cataloging-in-Publication Data
Boyle, Kay, 1902–
Process : a novel / by Kay Boyle ; edited and with an
introduction by Sandra Spanier.
p.   cm.
Includes bibliographical references.
ISBN 0-252-02668-3 (acid-free paper)
1. Young women—Fiction. 2. Mothers and daughters—
Fiction. 3. Cincinnati (Ohio)—Fiction. I. Spanier, Sandra
Whipple. II. Title.
PS3503.O9357P75   2001
813'.52—dc2   00-011853

IN GRATEFUL MEMORY

OF MY GRANDMOTHERS,

Nona Thompson Whipple (1896–1982)

AND

Esther Burley Lockwood (1897–1999)

— S . S .

ACKNOWLEDGMENTS

I am most grateful to Ian von Franckenstein, Kay Boyle's son and literary executor, for permission to publish this novel, to quote from her letters, and to use photographs from her personal collection and for his ongoing support of my work on his mother. For permission to publish the manuscript and quote from Boyle's letters to Louise Morgan Theis I am grateful to the Berg Collection of English and American Literature at the New York Public Library, Astor, Lenox, and Tilden Foundations. At the New York Public Library, Wayne Furman, Stephen Crook, Rodney Phillips, Philip Milito, and the staff of the Berg Collection have been helpful at all stages of this project. I am grateful, too, to Elaine Sproat, literary executor for Lola Ridge, for granting access and permission to quote from the Lola Ridge collection and for responding so generously to my queries. Paula Scott kindly provided permission to quote from letters by Evelyn Scott. I am indebted to Special Collections, Morris Library, Southern Illinois University at Carbondale, for permission to quote from the Kay Boyle Papers, and particularly to Katharine Salzmann for her continuous helpfulness on short notice. I am also indebted to the Rare Books and Manuscripts Division, Special Collections Library, the Pennsylvania State University Libraries to quote from Boyle's letter to Doug Palmer, with special thanks to Sandra Stelts for years of ready assistance. I owe thanks also to Linda Bailey at the Cincinnati Historical Society and to the staffs at the

Harry Ransom Humanities Research Center at the University of Texas at Austin, the Annenberg Rare Book and Manuscript Library at the University of Pennsylvania, the Beinecke Rare Book and Manuscript Library at Yale University, and the Sophia Smith Collection at Smith College. For research assistance I wish to thank Janet Holtman and Beth Widmaier, who also transcribed the typescript. I am grateful to my friends and colleagues at Penn State who have read portions of the manuscript, answered questions, and served as sounding boards: Bernard Bell, Deb Clarke, Cheryl Glenn, Kathryn Grossman, Susan Harris, William J. Harris, John Harwood, Jacqueline Rogers, Jack Selzer, James Smith, Susan Squier, and Stanley Weintraub. To Suzanne Clark, with whom I have shared many adventures in scholarship, I owe special thanks for the ongoing conversation. Graham Spanier has provided steady support and encouragement, and Brian and Hadley have helped keep things in perspective.

INTRODUCTION

On December 2, 1922, a suitcase was stolen at the Gare de
Lyon in Paris containing the only copies of everything
Ernest Hemingway had written during his past year's ap-
prenticeship as a struggling young expatriate writer. Later he pro-
fessed that it was probably for the best. Starting over, he had forged
a new style. But clearly the loss haunted him all his days, and it has
captured the popular imagination as well, even inspiring novels like
The Hemingway Hoax and *Hemingway's Suitcase.*[1] The recovery of Kay
Boyle's lost first novel, the manuscript missing since the 1920s and
published here for the first time, may not pack such star power. But
Process, written in 1924 and 1925 when Boyle was herself a young
American in France, is a significant addition to the body of early
twentieth-century American literature and potentially a pivotal text
for reassessing literary modernism.

The discovery of the manuscript was a scholar's dream. I was not
even looking for it when I came across the entry in the old-fashioned
oak card catalog in the hushed, high-ceilinged room of the New York
Public Library that houses the Berg Collection of English and American Literature. The aging index card read simply:

Boyle, Kay
Process. Typescript (carbon), unsigned and undated. 119 p.
Sent to Louise Morgan Theis.

I had been working on an edition of Kay Boyle's letters, a project she had authorized me to undertake in 1991, the year before her death at the age of ninety. Although she had never believed in publishing personal letters and deplored what she saw as a peculiarly American obsession with the private life of the artist, she was becoming aware of her place in literary history and wanted the record to be straight. I had written a book about her in 1986, the first devoted to her life and work, and had edited a volume of her short stories, and I think she trusted me not to sensationalize a life that was admittedly pretty sensational.[2] (In addition to writing more than forty books of fiction, nonfiction, and poetry, she had three husbands and raised eight children—six of her own and two stepchildren from the marriage of her second husband, Laurence Vail, to Peggy Guggenheim. And she knew everyone. In her address book the *B* page alone included such close personal friends as Samuel Beckett and Joan Baez.) That Saturday afternoon in February 1999, I decided to make one more pass through the card catalog to be sure that I had not missed any important items. I must have skimmed past the entry for the typescript on previous visits, but this time it caught my eye.

I knew that Boyle had corresponded in the 1920s with Otto and Louise Morgan Theis, both editors at the *Outlook*, a political and literary weekly published in London that folded in 1928. From Boyle's letters of the period, as well as her autobiographical accounts, I also knew that she had written a novel of her youth in Cincinnati (variously called "Source" and "Process"), and I knew that it had been lost. In her memoirs, *Being Geniuses Together, 1920–1930*, Boyle recalls that soon after her arrival in France in 1923, isolated with her young husband amid her new in-laws in a village in Brittany and speaking little French, she started work on the novel of her beginnings, "as if a recounting of these experiences must finally reveal to me who I was."[3] She writes that she finished the novel in the winter of 1924 in a squalid apartment in Le Havre. In a footnote she adds that in 1928 she gave her only copy of the book to Robert Sage, then associate editor of the little magazine *transition*, who gave it "in all good faith" to a Chicago publisher friend who mislaid the manuscript: "and it has never been heard of since" (*BGT* 129). The typescript I found had been processed by the New York Public Library in 1964—no other source information is on record. But we will return to the mystery of the missing manuscript.

As her friend Studs Terkel put it, Kay Boyle was *there*.[4] She had a knack for being in the midst of the defining events and movements of the twentieth century. Her literary life got underway in Greenwich Village in 1922 when she took a job as an assistant to Lola Ridge, the American editor of Harold Loeb's *Broom*—"probably the handsomest and arty-est of any literary publication of its time" (*BGT* 14)—and first met such life-long friends as William Carlos Williams and Marianne Moore. She had left home that spring and in June 1922 married Richard Brault, a French engineering student she had met back in Cincinnati who had followed her to New York City. In May 1923 Kay and Richard sailed for France to visit his family in Brittany, intending to be away for three or four months. He would get a temporary job and, as Boyle recalled, "I would begin my novel, and after the first few chapters were done, a New York publisher would pay me an advance so that I might finish it, and this would take care of our return fare" (*BGT* 39–40). Boyle would not return to the United States, however, for eighteen years. Her first published novel, *Plagued by the Nightingale*, did not appear until 1931.

Although technically not an expatriate, having been required by law to assume her husband's French citizenship, Boyle was very much a part of the legendary gathering of expatriate writers and artists in Paris in the 1920s. Her early poetry and fiction appeared in the avant-garde little magazines published in Paris alongside the work of James Joyce, Gertrude Stein, Ezra Pound, Djuna Barnes, Hart Crane, H. D., Williams, and Hemingway. Like many of her literary contemporaries, in the wake of the Great War she found herself chafing against the constraints of Main Street America in an era of conservatism and complacency, prosperity and Prohibition. Gertrude Stein famously called them a "lost generation." Art was what they had instead of God, and they took as seriously as a religious call Ezra Pound's rallying cry of modernism: "Make it new!"

But Boyle's career stretched decades beyond the expatriate twenties. In the thirties, living in Austria, England, and France, she witnessed and wrote of the rise of fascism in Europe, until war forced her home to America in 1941 in the company of her second husband,

Laurence Vail, his ex-wife, Peggy Guggenheim (with her future husband Max Ernst), and their combined family of six children. Traveling separately on a refugee ship was the man who would become Boyle's third husband, Joseph von Franckenstein, an Austrian baron who refused to live under Nazism when his country was annexed by Germany in 1938, whom Boyle met in Mégève, France, where he was a ski instructor and children's tutor. In the forties, Boyle's work appeared in mass-market magazines, and she published the first book about the French resistance; in 1944 the novel *Avalanche*, originally serialized in the *Saturday Evening Post*, became her only best-seller. From 1946 to 1952 she wrote fiction about occupied Germany as a foreign correspondent for the *New Yorker* until she fell victim to McCarthyism and was blacklisted for much of the fifties. In the sixties Boyle was a well-known Bay Area writer, teacher, and activist. She was arrested during a Vietnam War protest for blocking the entrance to the Oakland Induction Center and went to prison with Joan Baez and her mother. During the 1968 student strike at San Francisco State, she was publicly fired by university president S. I. Hayakawa. (The dismissal was invalid, and she got her tenure while she was in jail.) For the remaining three decades of her life she continued to speak out in print and in person in support of human rights and social justice. Even after moving to a Marin County retirement home in 1989, she organized an Amnesty International group, and she delighted in unsettling some of her fellow residents when she determined to integrate the dining room by inviting friends of color to lunch.

An active writer to the end, Boyle brought out a book in every decade of the twentieth century beginning in the twenties. Three books, including a complete revision of a 1933 novel and a new poetry collection, were published in 1991 alone, her eighty-ninth year. The sum of her work is a chronicle of the twentieth century. And she could claim a distinguished pedigree of literary honors, including O. Henry Awards for Best Short Story of the Year in 1935 and 1941, two Guggenheim Fellowships, honorary degrees, membership in the American Academy of Arts and Letters (where she occupied the Henry James chair), and a Senior Fellowship from the National Endowment for the Arts for her extraordinary contribution to contemporary American literature over a lifetime of creative work.

Boyle was born on February 19, 1902, in St. Paul, Minnesota. But hers was not a typical middle American childhood. Six months after her birth, her paternal grandfather, Jesse Peyton Boyle, the family patriarch and provider, broke off with his partners at the West Publishing Company, which he had helped found in 1882, and moved his family East. Kay spent her childhood living in and around Philadelphia, Washington, D.C., Atlantic City, and the Pocono Mountains of Pennsylvania. The family also spent time in Europe, where on her grandfather's fortune they "traveled expensively, and dined expansively, in a great many different countries" (BGT 19).

Her father, Howard Peterson Boyle, she describes as almost pathologically incompetent, ever in the shadow of his powerful and willful father. "Quite simply and tragically," she writes, "he knew he would fail in whatever he undertook to do."[5] During an extended period when her grandfather was ill and her father was left to manage by himself, the family's wealth began to dwindle. Jesse never laid blame on his son; his response to adversity was to draw up and proudly soldier on. Kay writes of her grandfather: "In some strange way, it was as if his spirits lifted each time my father failed, as if every new piece of evidence of his son's incompetence served to enhance his own authority."[6] In 1916 the family moved to Cincinnati, where Kay's father went into business with his cousin and established the Boyle Engineering Company, an auto repair shop in the city's industrial section. As their financial situation continued to deteriorate, the family lived in progressively more modest dwellings, finally moving into an apartment converted from storage space on the office floor above the garage. In a belt-tightening move, her father took over foreman duties in the shop: "There he put on a touching act of enormous energy, hastening aimlessly around, pad and pencil in hand, in mortal terror of every trucker who drove his rig in and ill-at-ease with the crew of five or six mechanics fate was asking him to supervise."[7]

On her mother's side, Boyle came from a strong line of independent women. She was proud that her grandmother, Eva S. Evans, had been one of the first women to work for the federal government. At the age of seventeen, she had married a Kansas schoolmaster, but in 1881 left her husband and took her two young daughters to Washington, D.C., where she worked at the Department of the Interior in the land-grant office, registering homesteading claims. One of those daughters, Nina Evans Allender, became an honorary co-chair of Alice Paul's militant National Woman's Party and a cartoonist for the party's magazine, the *Suffragist*. In 1921 her political cartoons were part of a Library of Congress exhibition marking ratification of the Nineteenth Amendment, and in 1934 her drawing of Susan B. Anthony appeared on a U.S. postage stamp.

The most powerful influence in Boyle's early life was her mother, Katherine Evans Boyle. "Because of my mother, who gave me definitions, I knew what I was committed to in life; because of my father and grandfather, who offered statements instead of revelations, I knew what I was against," she would write later. "I had the most satisfactory of childhoods," she says, "because Mother, small, delicate-boned, witty, and articulate, turned out to be exactly my age." Chronic ill heath had prevented her mother from receiving a formal education, "and so her spirit had remained fervent and pure" (*BGT* 18). Kay herself had little formal schooling. Her bouts with whooping cough and typhoid fever, coupled with the family's frequent moves and a traumatic first day at kindergarten when two bullies locked her in the cloakroom closet, led her mother to conclude that there would always be time in the years ahead for her education. Yet it was a most stimulating and literate childhood. In the evenings her mother would read aloud while Kay and her sister, Joan, two years older, drew illustrations for each book. At a dinner party in Philadelphia, her mother had read from Gertrude Stein's *Tender Buttons* and one of the guests laughed so hard that he had to be taken upstairs to bed. (The Stein reading was followed by excerpts from Kay's diary of her trip to Germany the previous summer.) In 1913, Katherine took her daughters to the landmark Armory Show in New York City, the introduction of modern art to America. There they saw the radically innovative works of artists such as Man Ray, Constantin Brancusi, Francis Picabia, and Marcel Duchamp, whose *Nude Descending a Staircase* sparked excitement and outrage. At the age of eleven Kay Boyle could not have imagined that in years to come she would be photographed in Paris by Man Ray, that Brancusi would leave his dog in her care, that Picabia would become the godfather of her firstborn child, or that Duchamp would be godfather to her last.

Kay Boyle photographed by her
mother, Katherine Evans Boyle,
Beach Haven, N.J., circa 1912.
(Collection of Sandra Spanier)

Katherine was a friend of Alfred Stieglitz, who revolutionized
photography as an art form and exhibited the work of many modern
artists, including his wife, Georgia O'Keeffe. In their long correspondence, Katherine would report on her daughters' artistic development, enclosing their poems and drawings along with her own
photographs of the girls. Paintings by Kay and Joan were included in
an exhibition of children's art at his legendary "291" Gallery in New
York. Invited by Stieglitz to contribute a statement for his magazine
Camera Work as to what his recently closed "291" had meant to her,
Katherine wrote in a letter of January 4, 1915, that she had rebelled
against suggestions of well-meaning friends that she find a teacher
to direct her daughters' talents: "'291' made me understand that to
allow my children to work out their ideas unconsciously, to allow
them the sanctity of their own imaginations—to permit them to be
themselves, was the greatest good I could render them."[8] Looking
back, Boyle would write of her mother in loving tribute, "She alone,

with her modest but untroubled intuitions about books and painting, music and people, had been my education" (*BGT* 18).

Boyle was brought up by her mother to believe that social activism and art went hand in hand. Running for the Cincinnati school board on the Farmer-Labor ticket in 1921, Katherine would read aloud to labor union organizers from James Joyce's *Ulysses* (then appearing in the *Little Review*) and show them reproductions of Brancusi's work, "untroubled in her belief that his 'Endless Column' would be accepted by them as a symbol for labor's enduring hope."[9] Among the earliest of Kay Boyle's writings to survive are her teenaged literary efforts, each clearly dated and neatly copied in a fair hand in a leatherbound notebook.[10] From July 1916 to May 1918—while her Aunt Nina was out west campaigning for votes for women, her mother was defying the men of the family by playing the recordings of her favorite German composers (at a time when German-sounding street names in Cincinnati were anglicized in a show of wartime patriotism), and America was reacting to the 1917 Russian Revolution in the first "Red Scare"—Boyle was turning out poems with titles like "The People's Cry," "For Children Work," "The Working Girls' Prayer," "The Battle Field," and "Young Russia."

In the fall of 1921, Boyle was working the switchboard at her father's garage business in Cincinnati, plotting her escape. She was growing increasingly impatient with the home scene, her eye on wider horizons. "I am worrying at present over the lack of literature in Soviet Russia," she wrote to Joan on November 9. "The only way that we can possibly get at the fundamentals of that great and glorious experiment is to hear what the youth of them is saying and conditions make it impossible, at the present time."[11] Joan had moved to New York and, through their mother's friendship with Frank Crowninshield, landed a job at *Vogue*. Kay, who had studied at the Conservatory of Music and taken part-time courses in architecture at the Ohio Mechanics Institute, had sold her violin to pay for a night course in secretarial school, wanting a "practical skill" that would enable her to get a job and earn enough to follow her sister east. She was indignant when a dictation exercise consisted of a letter from a mayoral candidate to an influential businessman extolling the Republican party and calling on his support "'to fight the growth of Socialism in this country and absolutely exterminate their unsound principles.'" "This to the ignorant young stenographers who have no ideas of their own and who will swallow it whole," she complained to Joan. "All the evil in the world starts in the schools. My dear, I am becoming more radical everyday. Absolutely *red*. I believe in nothing but beauty."[12]

Boyle was equally impassioned about the need for artistic revolution. That same month her first publication—a letter to the editor—appeared in Harriet Monroe's *Poetry: A Magazine of Verse.* In it Boyle deplored "the complacency of the reactionaries of the musical world" who insisted that music "should remain more than a little antiquated, scented with lavender while the contemporary arts are keeping pace with the complexities of civilization." Citing such innovative modern writers and artists as Sherwood Anderson, Amy Lowell, Picasso, and Brancusi, she argues with passion and aplomb: "Whether or not they gain a foothold is as much our concern as theirs, for they *are* ourselves, our explanation, the story which the future generations shall read of us. And meanwhile music stands like a Boston bas-bleu, her skirt a little shortened because of the influence of Korsakov and Dvorak, but still wearing her New England rubbers."

Meanwhile, at home relations were growing increasingly intolerable between "the allies" (herself, her mother, and her fiancé, Richard) and "the belligerent powers" (her father and her grandfather, nicknamed "Puss"—short for "Grand-puss"). "We must get away from here," she wrote her sister on December 12:

> I am losing all sweetness and good-will towards men. And poor mother has to go through more than you can imagine. Sometimes I could commit murder without a qualm. We sit at the table and every time mother opens her mouth you might think that a maniac was beginning to speak from the sweet and forbearing silence which immediately falls upon the masters of our house. . . . Why a liberal idea is a black and unforgivable sin, and the Indians can die like cattle in boxcars and the miners be killed in West Virginia, and the unemployed starve and yet we here must not talk of these things, but of Fatty Arbuckle. And Puss had the damned nerve to sit back in his chair the other night after gorging three bananas and five pastries and a dozen or so of doughnuts, pat himself comfortably and say: "Do you know Howard, I think there must be people starving in America today?" I said: "Think?", and left the table. He sickens me.

"I have got to get started in life and every day I spend here is time wasted," she declared.[13]

. . .

Kay Boyle's first novel captures this phase of her youth in all its passionate indignation and urgency to independence. *Process* is a classic *Bildungsroman*, a novel of development. More specifically, it is a *Künstlerroman*, an autobiographical account of the artist's origins—Boyle's counterpoint to James Joyce's *Portrait of the Artist as a Young Man*.

Like Joyce's Stephen Dedalus, Boyle's protagonist, Kerith Day, is a sensitive youth, self-consciously in search of her identity and her place in the world. In the course of the novel she reckons her position within the family and society that thus far have shaped her, and she rebels against the confines of her past and present existence. Unlike Joyce's young protagonist, a Roman Catholic with rigorous Jesuit training whose tormented struggle with his religious faith is central to his development, Kerith places her faith only in art and politics. And she is a woman of action in the material world. Allied with her artistically and politically progressive mother, Kerith moves in a sphere of Bohemian social relationships and radical labor activities, facing down the disapproving patriarchs. She is as contemptuous of their failures of imagination and emotion as of their conservative politics. In the course of the novel, Kerith explores her artistic, social, and personal values. She revels in her relationship with the sensuous natural world outside the Cincinnati city limits—a world that stands in sharp contrast to the grinding existence of the urban working class. She rejects a kindly but cerebral suitor and experiences a sexual awakening with a French student and kindred spirit. And ultimately, like Stephen Dedalus, she flies the nets of family, convention, and country to go abroad, determined to forge her own future.

Yet in a move that breaks with the pattern of traditional (predominantly male-authored) novels of development, in which maturation is measured by individuation and autonomy, Boyle sets her heroine on a path to maturity and selfhood that does not circumvent commitment and community. The novel ends with Kerith poised for flight, but not in isolation. The last we see her, she is linked in a threesome, holding hands with her mother and fiancé, laughing and running through the snow of Cincinnati's Eden Park, about to get away.

Process is a *roman à clef*, literally a "novel with a key," its charac-ters corresponding clearly to the people in Boyle's life. The resem-blances are unmistakable between Kerith Day and Kay Boyle, be-tween Kerith's physically fragile but forward-thinking mother and the author's own. Kerith's ineffectual and weak-spirited father, Har-ry Day (called H. D.), is much like Boyle's father, Howard Peterson (H. P.) Boyle. The formidable patriarch of the novel, Jesse Day, is clearly modeled after Boyle's grandfather, Jesse Peyton Boyle, "one of the few charming reactionaries" Boyle had ever encountered.[14] This fictional family, like Boyle's, has suffered a financial decline and lives in Cincinnati above an automotive repair shop and garage in quarters furnished with Persian rugs, Pekinese dogs, and other remnants of a previous life of taste and privilege. Like the Boyle fam-ily, the Days have lived the American Dream in reverse, moving from the moneyed class to the working class. Yet the grandfather's faith in the American capitalistic system and the Protestant work ethic re-mains undaunted. As had Kay, Kerith hurts her father and grandfa-ther by quitting her unpaid job at the switchboard of the family busi-ness to work as a stenographer to a wholesale jeweler in an effort to earn enough to buy her freedom. Kerith's intellectual suitor, Brod-sky, is likely modeled after Lewis Browne, a rabbinical student at the Hebrew Union College whom Boyle's mother hoped she would mar-ry. Boyle identifies Browne as "the leading male figure in my novel": "But he was not the adventure that I wanted; he was old (perhaps twenty-seven or twenty-eight) and crippled with rheumatism, and both his mind and flesh repelled me" (*BGT* 68).[15] Finally, Kerith's kindred spirit, Soupault, is clearly the fictional counterpart of Boyle's first husband, Richard Brault, a sardonic French veteran of World War I.

In 1929 Boyle joined a group of avant-garde expatriates who signed a thirteen-point manifesto published in the little magazine *transition* calling for the "Revolution of the Word." It proclaimed, among other things, "The writer expresses. He does not communi-cate" and "The plain reader be damned."[16] (By the 1970s her position had moved a full 180 degrees when she asked rhetorically of a young poet: "Writing *is* communication, isn't it?"[17]) In its idiosyncratic subject matter and innovative style, *Process* is challenging reading, but so are most of the acclaimed masterpieces of modernism. When

The Waste Land was published as a book after first appearing in the November 1922 issue of the *Dial*, T. S. Eliot added annotations and explanatory notes totaling nearly half the length of his poem. Following the publication of his monumental *Ulysses* (1922), James Joyce encouraged and assisted Stuart Gilbert in writing a book-length explication of the novel. Many of Gertrude Stein's works are commonly considered impenetrable. Like other cutting-edge works of its time, *Process* pushes the envelope of genre distinctions, blurring the boundary between fiction and poetry. This long-lost first novel is the purest, most sustained example we have of the high modernist Boyle. It is her germinal effort to "make it new."

The 1929 manifesto also proclaims, "Narrative is not mere anecdote, but the metamorphosis of reality." Decades later Margaret Atwood would describe the world Boyle creates in her fiction: "This is a solid world solidly described, but it is also a world in which matter is merely a form of energy." While Boyle's writing has sometimes been considered close to surreal, "there is nothing of the ant-covered clock about it. What it approaches instead is the hallucinatory, or rather the moment of visionary realism when sensation heightens and time for an instant fixes and stops."[18]

From its opening pages it is apparent that in this novel, language will take on a life of its own. The industrialized Cincinnati landscape is described in surprising metaphor: "Streets curl into the hills and wired inclines above them stand sharp like long-legged birds in fume. The hills lean away from the smoke, lean away from the river that cleaves them" (1). Kerith, driving fast and singing "a song against the city" (1), impulsively stops the car on a height, where she and her mother sit, smoke cigarettes, and exclaim at the sky, spread lovely over the rail yards and the "soiled short houses of factory workers" (2). Below them "the river sucked at the flat dull breast of Kentucky" (2).

Process demonstrates perhaps more clearly than any of her previously published work Boyle's early commitment to the "Revolution of the Word." In onomatopoetic language, she captures the "sullen plurp" (14) of coffee in the percolator and the sound of H. D.'s persistent typing, as the "machine tack-tacked on" (35). Both the hated switchboard that confines Kerith to the office and the sultry summer air are described as living things: "White eyes of the switchboard lolled upon the heat. A cool-beaked wind pecked at Kerith's throat, drooped away as though suddenly oppressed by the weight of heat" (17). Syntax is subordinated to sense in a sentence like this: "Twang of the switchboard hummed the heat" (9). Or this, when Kerith returns to the city after a day in the country only to be stopped and given a ticket by a traffic cop: "They drove down into the outskirts where drugstore windows bleared the corners, and from the intimacies of movie shows oozed a watery discharge of faces. Heat paunched up close at a crossing, jutted in a blue uniform, stopping the Ford with elbows on the window leaning in" (23).

Lyrical and episodic, the novel moves as much through implication and revelation as it does through plot.[19] The opening chapter establishes in elliptical dialogue and charged description the landscape and family dynamics that form the backdrop for Kerith's flight to freedom. It shows us the intimate bond between Kerith—a modern young woman who smokes, drives, and bobs her hair—and Nora, her mother, physically fragile but strong and sure in her convictions and quiet defiance of convention. Thinking of her father, in contrast, Kerith concludes, "We never happened to each other" (2). In an extraordinary reversal of fictional stereotypes, yet true to Boyle's experience, the mother in this novel acts not as an impediment but as an impetus in her daughter's quest for independence: "'I want you away from here,'" Nora tells her. "Her voice swayed the ripe phase of Kerith's life. Work in her father's office was without finality. It was his unending existence, but for her it ripened, it had grown heavy and was ready to drop away from her" (3). Our introduction to the men of the family is a glimpse of a sign from a distance, a telling visual image more powerful than explanation: "Through the arch and below them, electric letters 'JESSE DAY AND SON, Drive In' flashed back into the roofs, grew up gradually again, erect and frail" (3). Boyle captures character in deft strokes of description. When the grandfather speaks, "wind blustered his mustache" (5), and he walks down stairs "leaning back from the drag of his belly" (9).

Throughout the novel Boyle contrasts the sordid industrialized city with an idyllic natural world. But her rural landscapes are not pastoral cliches. Rather, her descriptions of the land, trees, waters, sky are dynamic, charged with an energy that is sometimes overtly erotic. She also challenges traditional distinctions between mind and body that privilege the intellect over instinct and emotion. Like the work of many modernists—D. H. Lawrence, Mabel Dodge Luhan, and O'Keeffe, who went to Taos and Santa Fe; Katherine Anne Porter and Hart Crane, who went to Mexico; Picasso and Stein, who found inspiration in African masks, or Stieglitz, who exhibited them in his gallery—this novel reveals a fascination, if not an idealization, of the "primitive" in reaction against modern urban mechanization.

In an episode vaguely reminiscent of one in Kate Chopin's *The Awakening* (1899), when the heroine escapes New Orleans to spend a luxuriant day simply eating and napping on a primitive island, Kerith and Brodsky take a drive in the country, stop at a black man's cabin, and taste his homemade liquor. Kerith idealizes his simple, harmonious life, inquiring gravely, "'You *are* free, aren't you?'" (18). But he resists being romanticized, responding that he pays his taxes like everyone else. As she watches him, Kerith admires his dignity and self-sufficiency: "His hands served them but his body was suspended. His back flowed into dark patterns of thew, tapering to raw stabs of light. Kerith felt the white stretch of her skin like a sterility upon her." She sees his eyes travel "to the cabin where the full rick leaned with barley, and gourds ripening against the dipping step were flushing a slow deep gold from green" (19). Yet his voice "exclude[s] her from the voluptuous harvest" (19); his eyes "approached and almost included her, and then closed back into his unshaken soul" (19).

Kerith becomes irritated with Brodsky's pronouncement that there can be no "material freedom" and that what matters is intellectual liberation: "Brodsky's cool white voice drew an impeccable line between mind and body" (19). Kerith rejects the division. In an animated and sensuous passage in which the whole universe seems sexually charged, Kerith wades into a stream, and the customary distinctions between subject and object, perceiver and perceived, mind and body dissolve:

> She walked away from them, down to the streaming water. The evening of pure blue glass splintered on flame, and the stream gully writhed barren of trees, dark vein of water bearing a scar of flame. Kerith's feet were blue-lipped under water, her gathered skirts bruised on her knees. White water spouted from her ankles. The stones were cold flesh on the palms of her feet.

Kerith felt the cold full touch of water and stone, the dark bushes against her like puffs of wind, restoring silence in her. She walked wonderingly up the land, watching the sky burn and pale to wax. She moved in the clear spaces between the firm-breasted bush feeling the miracle of restored silence in her. Presently wondering white lights of worms tingled out near the water, and below in the taper of the stream, river-birches were black and semen-podded against the clear pure wave of sky.

She walked slowly up, feeling herself in movement in the perfect un-fecundated womb. (19–20)

Unlike Kerith, Brodsky is not at home in his body. He is "clear and unconfused" (23) in his university learning, a "cool remote be-ing" (12). His pale flesh hangs "heavy and dull" (68), and when he walks his hands sway "heavy and obscene before him" (69). In con-trast, Soupault is a force of nature: brown, quick, lithe. He walks "with an animal-like indolence" (31), and his skin is "cool and im-mune like the gold belly of a snake" (46). He is "indifferent and ab-sorbed in the perfect unknown knowledge of his body" (31). Soupault has seen the destruction of bodies in war and knows the limitations of language: "It was so with trees, the dead withered bark of trees that was mute to everyone, and then stemming within, the clear flow of white vitality from the roots of life" (31). When Soupault lights Ker-ith's cigarette, she responds "with a full involuntary tremor": his "lean hard wrist, the lean curve of flesh into his sleeve, struck throb-bing notes of knowledge in her" (44). Boyle does not detail Kerith's sexual initiation with Soupault in the woods, but it is transforming, and she emerges arrogant and empowered.

Kerith entertains multiple points of view as she searches to find her own way. She is willing to listen to her Rotarian employer wax el-oquent about his belief in "the realization of ideal service, and in self-realization through service" (41) until his callous disregard for conditions in his own jewelry factory leads to a worker's death. While she is sympathetic to radical labor, she is exasperated by the limited imaginations of workers who respond more enthusiastically to Wil-liam Z. Foster's promises of rest homes, variety shows, and a higher rung on the power ladder than to Lincoln Steffens's call for the cre-ation of an entirely new system of values. What she will not tolerate is indifference. When Soupault claims he is attending a rally at the Labor Temple simply because he has nothing better to do and asserts that individual efforts make no difference, she slaps his face.

When Kerith knows it is time to set off on her own, she quits her job and declares herself free forever from "false work": "She would never work again for conditions as they were" (86). Her epiphany is not merely spiritual but physical. She feels her hands "long and hard before her like miraculous instruments": "'I am the miracle,' she said looking into her hands, 'I am the perfect ego released'" (87). She goes straight to tell Soupault, who declares he will join her, and the vows they exchange are hardly the traditional ties that bind:

> "We'll just go away together," said Soupault.
> "Until the time comes to go on to something else," she said. (88)

In striking contrast to the symbolism in most women's novels of awakening, Kerith's silver engagement ring is not an emblem of confinement but of opportunity: it is simply a way out that her father and grandfather can understand. In her memoirs, describing her youthful rebellion of the twenties from the vantage point of San Francisco in the sixties, Boyle wrote of her marriage to Brault:

> Our life together was going to be a confirmation of our impatience with conventions and our commitment to something called freedom in which we believed so passionately (the terms as contemporary and familiar as that). . . . We knew what we were about, and perhaps the clarity of our vision would reveal something fresh and new to them—they who had handed us the unspeakable horror of a world war and its aftermath and made no apologies about this gift. In a country that did not put its socialists in jail, as Eugene Debs was jailed in America, and did not harass its writers, as Upton Sinclair was harassed, I was going to write a novel in the quiet and peace of alien Brittany, and Richard was going to work his future out. (*BGT* 13–14)

Process is that novel, and it is unusual and noteworthy in American modernist writing for its simultaneous assertion of radical politics and radical poetics. Boyle was as active in the radical labor movement in Cincinnati as a teenaged girl could be. In the winter of 1923–24, having just finished a long poem called "The Book of Cincinnati" and at work on her novel, she sought a grant from the Garland Fund, established by the son of Marie Tudor Garland, a wealthy Greenwich Village patron of the arts. Charles Garland used his million-dollar inheritance to establish the Personal Service Fund "for individuals working creatively for society along radical lines," according to the letterhead stationery. Roger Baldwin, founder of the American Civil Liberties Union, was a trustee. Boyle needed a few hundred dollars for a return visit to New York to place her novel and work with Lola Ridge to establish a new magazine. Lola Ridge had quit *Broom* with the January 1923 issue in a dispute over the inclusion of a piece by Gertrude Stein, whose aesthetic experimentation she felt was divorced from meaningful contact with the social world. In a "breathless" letter to Ridge of January 26, 1923, Boyle, just twenty years old, expressed her devotion to Ridge and to a vision of artistic and political revolt as allied movements. She envisioned a new magazine that would "truly be the articulation of youth—youth, I mean, as we recognize youth in the spirit of the conscientious objector, the Irish Nationalists, the students of Germany, the Indian rebels—in every movement, the lucid magnificence of youth, against the dimmed false sentiment of age."[20]

On the last day of 1923, Boyle outlined her Garland Fund case in a letter to Ridge. She made only modest claims for her radical activities but she clearly saw her writing as a contribution to the movement:

> I worked all day, and at night my little Ford was at the command of the Farmer-Labour Party or any other radical organization which needed to be transported from one place to another or needed literature loaded or distributed. During the campaign of the Farmer-Labour Party in 1921 (I was then only eighteen) I drove the speakers night after night from street corner to street corner, distributed literature among the crowds, etc. Had I been older I might have done some actual work for them. In the winter of 1921 we had a huge mass meeting for Lincoln Steffens and William Z. Foster at the Labour Temple, at which I was head of the women ushers and sold badges and collected money. Chauffeured for Steffens and had a most interesting contact with him. But all this is unimportant technically. The only organization I belonged to was the Federated Press, and while Duane Swift spent several weeks in Cincinnati speaking at the different locals of the unions, I was with him constantly, driving the car and distributing blanks and literature, etc. Also spent weeks filling a very long petition for the Debs pardon. But this, as you can see, is entirely too scrappy, and that's all

there is to my radical career. The most important thing about me in that respect seems to me to be the fact that I've written the Book of Cincinnati, which is a specific and clear stroke of protest, and the fact that the book upon which I am now working is also of Cincinnati, is statedly in Cincinnati, Ohio, and besides being autobiography pure and simple is in its background of labour conditions in Cincinnati—and no one before has really taken the trouble to write about that nest of reactionary stagnation.

Ridge took up Boyle's case with the administrators of the Garland Fund, writing eloquently on her behalf. "The artist has been an isolated figure in every age. In our present industrial civilization, the revolutionary artist is doubly alone," she wrote to the fund's secretary, Anna N. Davis, on March 8, 1924. She sent a copy of Boyle's long poem and hoped they would give the case of "this young and gifted girl" their sympathetic consideration. Ridge wrote directly to her friend Roger Baldwin, saying of Boyle, "She has been filled since childhood with a passionate sympathy for radical labor, and with an indignation that has been expressed both in her work and in social action against all forms of exploitation and oppression. . . . She is a rare and unselfish spirit—one of the givers and one of the fighters."

The Garland Fund turned down the appeal. As Davis wrote to Ridge on March 12, 1924, from headquarters in the tony suburb of Brookline, Massachusetts: "It is curious that this poem of Kay Boyle's which you have sent, affects Roger Baldwin and me in just the same way. We may be very old-fashioned but to us it seems as though her words buried reality. The words themselves are often vivid, often beautiful, but we do not get down through them to much of any real substance. I am so sorry. The limitation may be entirely ours, and yet we may be representative of the 'general public'; and, if so, this writing, while it may be good as art cannot lay claim to help the radical movement." Presumably they were looking for social realism. A year later, in a letter to Ridge of January 25, 1925, Boyle would refer to the effort as the "Roger Baldwin fiasco."

Ironies abound. In 1924 she was not considered a true radical—disqualified by her devotion to revolutionizing the word as well as the world. And in the socially conscious thirties, her experimental work was dismissed by some critics as shows of mere stylistic virtuosity on "trivial" subjects. (This was written of her 1934 novel *My Next Bride*, another autobiographical coming-to-consciousness story, in which a young American woman in Paris trapped in a cult-like commune suffers a mental collapse, undergoes a back-street abortion, and is rescued through her friendship with another woman.) Yet in the forties—just as her work was becoming less experimental and more overtly polemic, taking as its subject matter the rise of fascism, resistance activities, and daily life in wartime France—critical tastes changed. The yardstick for significant fiction was recalibrated. With the New Criticism that came to dominate literary studies for several decades, art was to be considered apart from any biographical, social, or political context, and works expressing earnest passion and conviction, personal or political, were in danger of being downgraded from the category of high art to "sentimentality" or propaganda. In the fifties, Boyle became a victim of McCarthyism for her supposedly radical activities, beliefs, and associations.

Boyle's belief in the dual cause of aesthetic and political progressiveness is played out in *Process.* She was aware even then that it was a precarious position. In the novel, Kerith's mother hosts a workers' meeting, at which a collection is taken up for the defense of Nicola Sacco and Bartolomeo Vanzetti, the Italian immigrants and anarchists accused in a Boston murder case whose 1921 trial and conviction, long imprisonment, and execution in 1927 galvanized both artistic and political liberals. Yet the workers are suspicious of the ambiance in the apartment above the garage, furnished not only "with Turkey rugs and swell dogs" (12) but also with a Buddha on a gilded altar, incense sticks, and a brilliant square of silk to drop "where color was wanted" (44) or to take up when the mood strikes for an Isadora Duncan–like dance. "Kerith thought of the room bare, chairs and no hangings at the windows. *That* the men could have accepted without confusion" (27). "'But it doesn't seem these things goes with the labor movement'" one man says, pointing to Brancusi reproductions hanging on the wall. "'These pictures here. They don't mean anything to us.'" But Nora springs to correct his misconception and lament the destructive division between art and activism: "'Yes, oh, yes!' cried Nora. 'You're wrong. That's just what's wrong everywhere. Everyone concentrated, concentrated, and that's where the change has got to come. You haven't time for art and the artists are concentrated in themselves. That's where the change must come.'" Brancusi and the labor movement are "'deeply, deeply unit-ed,'" she tells them: "'He produces this and there are people just as ready to call him a criminal as there are people to cry out on a Lenin or any of your radical thinkers'" (13). The revolution she envisions is all-encompassing, bigger than most have yet imagined.

Soupault supplies the European perspective on art and politics. Spotting Kerith outside the Labor Temple, where black and red signs announce speeches by Foster and Steffens, he asks if she is "'with the workers.'" When she responds that she is "'with the radicals,'" he asks bemusedly: "'And in America the radicals and the workers are not one thing?'" (11). When she explains that in America the workers are largely opposed to the radicals, he can only laugh, and she feels "his mind alert and amused" (11). Decades later, in a *New York Times Book Review* interview called "Paris Wasn't Like That," Boyle noted that in the European tradition artistic and political expression were not separate matters. She emphasized her affinity for writers with whom she shared a political awareness: Anatole France; Emile Zola; Alexander Berkman and Emma Goldman, whom she knew in France; her friend Samuel Beckett, who had been active in supporting the French Resistance; and Albert Camus, who believed that the writer has an obligation to speak for those who cannot.[21]

Modernism as Kay Boyle first knew it was a broad, international movement. In the pages of *Broom* (subtitled *An International Maga-zine of the Arts*), she would have read the work not only of emerging American writers such as E. E. Cummings, Wallace Stevens, Malcolm Cowley, Hart Crane, Matthew Josephson, Jean Toomer, Waldo Frank, Evelyn Scott, Amy Lowell, Williams, and Stein but also of European writers in translation. In its brief lifetime (1921–24), *Broom* also published Fyodor Dostoyevski, Louis Aragon, Jean Cocteau, and in-stallments of "The Lay of Maldoror" by the Comte de Lautréamont (which Brodsky quotes at length in *Process*). The magazine featured the visual arts as well: photographs by Ray, drawings and paintings by Pablo Picasso, Juan Gris, Franco Modigliani, and Henri Matisse, and woodcuts on the cover by the Italian Futurist Enrico Prampolini.

In *Being Geniuses Together* Boyle pays homage to the writers and works that moved her. Upon her arrival in France in June 1923, the customs inspectors rigorously searched her baggage for "God knows what treasures," carelessly casting aside the treasures that were there: Lola Ridge's poetry collection *Sun-up* (1919), Morton Schamberg's photograph of her mother tucked inside a catalog from Alfred Stieglitz's "291" gallery, and first editions of works by Pound, Eliot, and Williams (*BGT* 43). She also carried George Moore's 1916 novel *The Brook Kerith*—a fictional rendition of the life of Jesus and most likely the inspiration for the name of Boyle's autobiographical protagonist. The first book she bought that summer in France was Raymond Radiguet's *Le Diable au Corps*, and she, who claimed to dislike reading and speak French not at all well, suddenly did both, transformed by the "magic lucidity" of Radiguet's prose. A few years later, after Radiguet's death in 1923 at the age of twenty, Caresse Crosby would ask her to translate the novel into English for the Black Sun Press, "not knowing that this book had led me out of the bleak silence of that summer in Brittany into the clarity of speech again" (*BGT* 69–70).

· · ·

In her first months in France, "I lived for the letters that Mother and Lola wrote me, and for the writing of letters to them" Boyle recalls (*BGT* 67). Her circle of correspondents gradually widened to include others: Williams, the Italian-American poet Emanuel Carnevali, and Evelyn Scott, a writer from the American South whose work was well known and highly regarded. It was Scott who read the manuscript of *The Sound and the Fury* by a little-known writer in Oxford, Mississippi, and recommended it to Harrison Smith and Jonathan Cape, who published her Civil War novel, *The Wave*, in 1929. When Faulkner's book came out later that year, a publicity blurb read, "*The Sound and the Fury* should place William Faulkner in the company of Evelyn Scott." When Faulkner was asked in 1940 whether there were any good women writers, he reportedly replied, "Well, Evelyn Scott was pretty good, for a woman."[22]

Through Boyle's letters of the period, in addition to her published memoirs and autobiographical writings, we can trace the genesis and progress of the novel and gain insight into her artistic aims and assessments of her work. Soon after her arrival in Brittany, finding herself nearly smothered in the bosom of Richard's family, she confided to Lola Ridge on June 20, 1923, that she had been sick, her thoughts restless and wanting action. "But I have begun to write a book, and it has helped a lot." The family was "dear and devoted," but "their conversation and reactions make me impatient," she said. "They feel that if I am left to myself for five minutes that I shall feel myself neglected. But whenever the darling Richard is here to keep them off, I write. . . . Oh, the situation is all primed for good production, Lola, my love, and I expect to write a lot." Over the summer she completed a long poem called "Book of Cincinnati," worked on translating Apollinaire's "Alcools," and set aside her novel to write short fiction. "I have dropped Kerith for awhile," she wrote her mother on August 21, 1923, "she is too utterly without a sense of humor."[23]

In the fall, Richard took a job with the electric company, and they took up residence in a squalid flat in the port town of Le Havre, "and there, as if it were the most natural thing in the world, we became members of the proletariat" (*BGT* 121). "I am *mad* to write," she wrote her mother on October 23, and looked forward to "a re-commencement of my novel."[24] On November 8 she told Ridge that she had only three chapters written, but she intended to finish the book that winter. By November 21 she reported to her sister, "Dearest, *how* I am writing. Kerith is getting bloody with reality—a poem has emerged, inchoate at present." She was incensed that her grandfather had written that she must be paid for her work, and she deplored his sentimentalization of their poverty: "He thinks of me mooning on sand-dunes, returning to a sweet little abstract apartment, Richard helping with the dishes—all on 30 cents a day. . . . One is liable to get raped or pneumonia on the dunes, we have nothing but oil-cloth—ripped cracked oil cloth that never stays clean—on our floors, not one easy chair, five days out of the week one can't use the middle room because the week's wash is up and *never* dries—consequently one leaps from puddle to puddle on one's way from bedroom to kitchen." But if she told him the truth, "he'd call me a pessimist—just because I can't philosophize and idealize and say soft lovely tearful brave things. And don't I know better than he how the body shivers beneath the fired brain but wouldn't I rather shiver and write what I want about life and the capitalistic system than have my remarkable 'earning power' amazing three continents? God damn it."[25]

"It turned out to be quite an intellectual winter," she later recalled. She read D. H. Lawrence's *Studies in Classic American Litera-*

ture and Norman Angell's *The Conditions of Allied Success*, which she rewrote in verse in order to understand. And she read and reread, "like a textbook," Rebecca West's *The Judge*: "All that mattered to me was that she was a woman, and that she had written a novel, a very long novel, which was what I was seeking to do" (*BGT* 144–45). Her mother regularly sent the *Dial*, the *New Republic*, *The Nation*, and the *Liberator*. For Christmas she sent Waldo Frank's *Holiday* and Evelyn Scott's autobiography *Escapade*, Scott's account of her elopement to Brazil with a married man, their poverty and isolation, and her experiences of childbirth and motherhood. "I think *Escapade* one of the most exciting and altogether tremendous things that has happened in America—the finest thing since O'Keeffe's exhibition last spring. I was mad with a tense wild recognition for weeks after finishing it," she wrote to Ridge on December 31. "I am so deeply thrilled with its beauty and strength." *Holiday* was "a decided anti-climax," and she diagnosed Waldo Frank as "a mystic attempting to save the world through realism" though he was in no way a realist.

After the Garland Fund turned her down, she wrote to Ridge on April 1, 1924, that her efforts had meant a great deal, but she now knew that she would not really want to return to New York. "Coming to France had meant to me the assertion of a new faith and the beginning of a new tradition. It has begun, and now the material expression of it must be solved," she wrote. "It is our bodies that live and even though our minds be free, if our bodies are living in protest, we are subservient. So I want to get my body away, out of the accepted basis of life and into its own reality. Here am I in our little room shrieking this at the skylight! I shall be free!" Her novel was in its second revision. When it was finished she hoped to "look for an isolate little house here on the sea and determine this thing in our souls: I believe in this, Lola—I believe it can be done. . . . The assertion of the artist spirit, without pose or sentimentality, to the progressive spirit of civilization."

In a letter of May 12, 1924, she reports to Ridge that her poem "Harbor Song" is finished (it would be published in *Poetry* in a censored version by Harriet Monroe, who did not feel she could risk the word *buttocks* or a section called "Whore Street"). "My book 'Source,' is practically done too, as well as several short stories," she wrote. The letter gives insight into her views on other modernist writers and into the experimental narrative method of her first novel, which reads much like poetry:

> I do feel too that there's something quite strange about all the young moderns who are writing. They seem to be mortally afraid of getting away from the center of action, from their cliques. They seem to go all to pieces when they are weeded out from the central poles of action in New York and Paris and are tossed aside to grow by themselves. As for me, I'm damned glad to be away—and I've written more than ever before, and I think it's worthwhile, Lola, I really do. I don't believe I'll write all summer. I want to discover a lot of possible poetic forms. There's a blank space in my soul where the inclination used to be to break poems up into different length lines, etc. The logical thing seems to be the paragraph form—and I think you are right, that it can be used only for certain things. So I must determine how I can say the rest of the things inside me.

She concludes, "When my novel is done, Lola darling, may I send you a copy for your hardest criticism, and if you think it's any good, would you recommend it somewhere?"

In the spring of 1924 Kay and Richard moved inland to Harfleur, and by the end of the summer the novel was nearly finished. "I want your reading of my book," she wrote to Ridge on August 11. "I feel this way about it. That compared to most other books, it is good—and that individual chapters are excellent—but compared with what there was within me seeking outlet, it is not a success. My people are not real—and in my mind they were not symbols of conflicting forces, but individuals. I have fundamentally failed. I want so much to know what you get out of it. I am not considering it for publication, but when I get time to type a copy I want you to see it and write me all you think of it."

In September she met Evelyn Scott in Paris. Scott's friend Louise Morgan Theis was also there, over from London—in the next few years, she, too, would become one of Boyle's friends and correspondents. On September 25, 1924, Boyle wrote to Ridge that her meeting in Paris with the Scotts had been delightful and reported: "I am typing the final version of my book PROCESS. If you are in New York and well, I want to send you a copy and see if any publisher would touch it. . . . I want your opinion of it, and I know its faults, but I have come to feel with Radiguet that the only thing of importance is the contemporary record of the aesthetic mind, and if I have outgrown the book, it at least reflected the process of that phase of development." In the meantime, Scott was writing to Ridge, waxing enthusiastic about Boyle, who had loaned her Williams's *Great American Novel* and Aldous Huxley's *Antic Hay* (and a few months later would loan her a rare copy of Joyce's *Ulysses*). She had not yet read all of Boyle's book, but she suspected that Boyle would be one of the truly great artists of her generation. She elaborated in two typewritten pages of effusive praise and critical analysis. Ridge's influence on Boyle was clear, as was that of Alfred Stieglitz, which was her only concern—she found the "piety" of his school irritating and asked Ridge to please try to save Boyle from youthful worship of "the old rabbi."[26]

"I have not wanted to write you until I could enclose the book, and here it is as a sort of Christmas greeting to you," Boyle began her letter to Ridge of December 15, 1924. She had just received a letter from Scott suggesting that Ridge might recommend the book to Thomas Seltzer (who would publish Scott's *The Golden Door* in 1925).[27] Scott also had offered to write a letter to Seltzer to be presented with the book. If that failed, Scott suggested that Ridge might get Waldo Frank to show the book to Horace Liveright. "Evelyn's enthusiasm simply floored me," Boyle wrote to Ridge, and she could not resist quoting Scott's response at length: "'Your book certainly is without question the best first novel in an immediate and personal sense that has ever been shown to me. That is the comparative judgement. But it [is] not only comparatively fine, but seems to me something to be remarked on for itself with that respect which the public at large only accedes to the classic.'" Scott placed Boyle's book in the company of recent novels by Williams, Cummings, and Frank and found them lacking in comparison. They were fine when they wrote "'poetically, in poetry undiluted,'" but when they got into "'the novelistic vein,'" they failed to make their characters distinguishable from one another. Scott told her: "'You are the only one who can be categoried in this group—who has the modern sense of the beautiful as a palpable subjective sensorial texture, who has also a capacity to preserve the persistent oppositions as in a fugue of individuals, individuals who are not simply the novelist in fancy dress, but who, though the novelist has taken them to her and they stem out of an identity in her emotions, keep their own consistent melodies.'"

Boyle was elated by the praise and eager for Ridge's response to her novel. She adds in a postscript: "Lola dear—this is my *original* copy—I have badly done carbons—but this is the *only one* I have to present to publishers."

But Seltzer did not take Boyle's novel for publication. "It was bound to happen," Boyle wrote Ridge on March 12, 1925. "*Please* don't worry about it. I get much more kick out of having you and Evelyn reacting to my things than anything else. But please sometime write me what you did think of 'PROCESS'—granted that it is little more than the hectic outburst of untrammeled youth."

To this point, the story of the manuscript's fate seems straightforward, but then the paper trail begins to fade. Once Seltzer had turned down the novel, Lola Ridge apparently gave it to Waldo Frank to show to Horace Liveright. In an undated letter from Frank to Ridge, probably written in the spring of 1925, he reports that he had not yet had time to read the novel, but that there would be no time lost because Liveright's principal reader, to whom he would give the manuscript, was in Europe. This "principal reader" was likely Otto Theis, who became Liveright's European agent in 1930 but was in contact with him earlier. And all we know of the provenance of the typescript of the novel in the New York Public Library's Berg Collection is the notation "Sent to Louise Morgan Theis."

But Boyle could just as well have given the manuscript to Louise Morgan Theis herself. Following a visit with the Theises in London, she wrote to Louise on July 11, 1925, from Harfleur, "We're safely arrived and quite wordless with gratitude for all your and Otto's gentillesse. You made it a most perfect time and the profoundest thing that I have got from it is that I shall presently re-write both my books." On October 20, 1925, she wrote to Theis, "Please, please, don't show the novel you have to anyone, and I know you wouldn't mind throwing it away, would you, because I've re-written it since and I have a horror of the first version, and someone or other is looking at it in New York with an encouraging look. Use the back for scrap paper."[28] The next day, on October 21, she wrote to Ridge: "To think that I haven't written you in gratitude for all the trouble you took over the old novel and your very fine criticism which was just what I needed, and so I re-wrote the damned thing and mother has it to give to you. Darling, do read it again, if you can, but don't think about it in any but a personal way. I'm doing better work now and I just want to know if you think it improved."

By that point, Boyle was deeply immersed in her second novel and about to begin her brief but intense relationship with Ernest Walsh, editor of *This Quarter,* who had published a poem and story of hers along with Hemingway's "Big Two-Hearted River" in the magazine's first issue. There is no further mention of *Process* in her letters. Ailing that winter in the cold climate, Boyle early in 1926 accepted Walsh's invitation to see his lung specialist in Paris and then join him and his coeditor, Ethel Moorhead, to recuperate in the south of France. Boyle's health quickly improved in the warmth and sun, and it was not long before she and Walsh fell in love. Walsh died of tuberculosis in October 1926, and in March 1927 Boyle gave birth to their daughter.

In the period of her bereavement, pregnancy, and new motherhood, Boyle's correspondence with Scott intensified. Louise Morgan Theis had a baby boy the same week Boyle gave birth to Sharon, and their friendship and correspondence continued. Richard Brault generously urged Boyle to bring the baby and join him in Stoke-on-Trent, England, where his new job had taken him, and she began to see Louise and Otto Theis on trips to London. After the publication of the first installment of *Plagued by the Nightingale* in *This Quarter* in 1927, Boyle's reputation began to soar. She was thrilled when Boni and Liveright asked to see the manuscript (the publisher would turn it down), and she got a letter of effusive praise from Williams (who would review her first book, *Short Stories,* when it was published in Paris by the Black Sun Press in 1929).[29] But Scott alludes to *Process* once more in a letter to Waldo Frank on December 21, 1931, following the publication—finally—of *Plagued by the Nightingale,* which she had recommended to the readers of the *Herald Tribune.* Boyle, she said, "whose first mss. I offered (and failed to sell) writes in a lyric strain and with a finish that no 'popular' American novelist can boast."[30]

A few mysteries remain. How did the typescript at the New York Public Library get into the papers of Louise Morgan Theis? Was it by way of Waldo Frank, Lola Ridge, Evelyn Scott, or Kay Boyle herself? Is the typescript the first version—which Boyle asked Theis to use for scrap paper—or the second, rewritten version, a copy of which Boyle had sent to Ridge via her mother in October 1925? The typescript in the Berg Collection is a carbon—what happened to the original? The return address on the manuscript is Kay Boyle, La Chartreuse, 10, rue des Caraques, Harfleur (S. I.), France. But the address cannot help us date the manuscript precisely. Boyle lived there from the spring of 1924 until early 1926—through the completion of the first version as well as the rewrite. And what of her story of the lost manuscript in *Being Geniuses Together*—that in 1928 she had given it to Robert Sage, who had given it to a Chicago publisher who had mislaid it? Is *that* where the original went? Or did she simply misremember? Her memoirs are not entirely accurate in every detail. She writes in *Being Geniuses Together* that she had sent her first novel, entitled *The Imponderables*, to Evelyn Scott, "and the brilliance and the ruthlessness of her criticism so excited me that I began the book again at the beginning, and I wrote it entirely over" (*BGT* 152). I have never found mention in any correspondence of any manuscript by that name, though her account of her determined revision rings true.

But Boyle was well aware of the limitations of memory and the "constructedness" of autobiography. In fact, she was more honest in her awareness than most. Throughout *Being Geniuses Together* she reminds us that she is reconstructing a story. She begins another autobiographical account with this admission and disclaimer: "There is no way for even the most honest among us to look into memory's dreamy, evasive eyes and know she can be persuaded not to lie, not to betray."[31] We may never know every answer to every question, but the answers do not change the importance of the novel published here.

. . .

Process represents an important missing piece in our knowledge and understanding of literary modernism. In its melding of avant-garde aesthetics and activist ethics, this novel belies the critical commonplace that literary modernism is apolitical, if not right-leaning with tendencies to fascism. It also supplies a critical missing piece in the history of the political novel in American literature, which so far has focused mainly on work of the thirties and beyond. *Process* makes individual consciousness the site of any meaningful social change. The personal is political—in a tradition traceable back through Emma Goldman's anarchic coupling of free speech and free love in her magazine *Mother Earth* to Harriet Beecher Stowe's appeal to individual conscience in her abolitionist novel *Uncle Tom's Cabin*. Boyle's first novel is not a polemic (though she would write many in years to come). But as an American modernist work, it is significant for its assertion that in the fragmented world of the early twentieth century, the individual struggle for self-definition and self-expression is bound up with the collective struggle for social justice.

At the same time, the novel presents a vision of mechanized modernity's despoiling of the natural world that should intrigue readers with an interest in environmental issues. In the sensual if not bawdy scene of the railroad workers' outing, Boyle politicizes the vision as she places labor, not management, in a sympathetic relationship with the land. Yet the novel celebrates one technology: the automobile. Ironically, Kerith's Ford is her means of escape from the industrialized city back to nature. No one but E. E. Cummings in his poem that starts

> she being Brand
> -new;and you
> know consequently a
> little stiff

has written about a car in such sexualized terms as does Boyle when describing Kerith playing chicken with a locomotive in her Ford and stopping the car just in time, knowing "that it was the bond and belief and pure subjection between herself and the car that had willed them into stopping. She might have sat there, she thought, and not lifted a finger, and yet the car would have stopped because it was in perfect response to her, and she was the attractile body drawing it to her direction and will" (73–74). If Kerith were an adolescent male, we might have expected this; that this describes a woman driver is extraordinary.

We have a canon full of novels of development written by men, but *Process* offers us a rare portrait of the artist as a young woman. As a portrait of an American as well as a female artist, it is an important counterpoint to the autobiographical first novels of some of her modernist contemporaries, including Joyce's *Portrait of the Artist as a Young Man*, Virginia Woolf's *The Voyage Out*, and F. Scott Fitzgerald's *This Side of Paradise*. And it is a significant addition to the body of work of other modernist American women like H. D., Evelyn Scott, Katherine Anne Porter, and Djuna Barnes.

Kerith's quest turns up more questions than answers, but Boyle is unflinchingly honest about the ambiguities, contradictions, and costs involved in her idealistic search for a new order. In the course of the novel Kerith looks to others as models of possible ways to live, but ultimately she concludes that she must tap her own source of meaning within herself alone and that every individual must strive first to honest self-awareness: "If I don't believe in my own experience," Kerith says, "I am lost" (87). Kerith's ways of knowing are corporeal and instinctual—she mistrusts the dispassionate intellect—so perhaps it is not surprising that the nature and even the aims of her rebellion defy easy explanation.

As the title would indicate, this novel depicts the heroine's process of coming of age and coming to consciousness of her identity. But since Boyle wrote it during a time when she had become "so totally French" that she barely recognized her reflection in a mirror (*BGT* 146), the title raises the intriguing possibility of a double entendre. The word *procès* in French means not only "process" but also "trial" or "inquisition." The French feminist theorist Julia Kristeva has played on the word, speaking of the *sujet en procès*—simultaneously meaning both "subject in process" and "subject on trial."[32] In this novel either meaning would apply.

Process is an almost startlingly innovative work. In this first novel Boyle blithely disregards the customary boundaries—between poetics and politics, mind and body, subject and object, perceiver and perceived, self and other—rupturing dichotomies in all directions. Even within a single category—radical labor politics on one end of the spectrum, the unabashed religion of capitalism on the other—she does not shy away from complication. Although her sympathies are with the workers, they are not all noble or enlightened. Rebekah, the feminist lawyer who fought for the federal amendment, disappoints Nora when she compromises her principles to advance her husband's and her own career. And while Boyle despises what they stand for, she represents the unreconstructed reactionaries of her novel, the Rotarian jeweler and especially the father and grandfather, with touches of understanding, pathos, even love. Her willingness to represent contradiction and complication has not made her an easy writer to pigeonhole or an obvious champion for a single cause, and in the course of her career this may have worked to her disadvantage.

Process wonderfully complements Boyle's published memoirs and her autobiographical early fiction, providing the prequel to her first four published novels, all drawn from her life in France in the 1920s: *Plagued by the Nightingale* (1931), *Year Before Last* (1932), *Gentlemen, I Address You Privately* (1933), and *My Next Bride* (1934). It is interesting to speculate what its impact might have been had *Process* been published when it was written, at a time when Boyle's star was on the rise and Katherine Anne Porter called her one of the "most portentous" talents of their generation.[33] Readers and critics of the twenties would have been receptive to the subject matter of the self-conscious individual quest for meaning and to the modernist narrative innovations that later would be dismissed as virtuosity or even preciosity by some critics of the next decade, when Boyle's expatriate novels finally appeared in print.

"I find it very convenient to have the same feelings now that I had when I was about eight or nine because I don't have to deny anything I ever wrote and say I didn't mean that" Boyle said in her late sixties.[34] In the 1980s she recalled her first novel as "a political novel, bringing in the Farmer-Labor party, Lincoln Steffens, and other political radicals whom Mother knew, as well as my own revolt against the men in our family, and my contempt for their views." "I'm sure it's just as well that it was lost," she adds, "but I speak of it here to emphasize that my views—and my writing—were always consistent to the point that I sometimes wonder if I do not suffer from arrested development."[35] The rediscovery of this first novel proves Kay Boyle right about her consistency but wrong about the novel's value and interest.

NOTES

1. Hadley Hemingway was joining her husband in Lausanne, where he was covering the peace conference as a journalist for the *Toronto Star,* and had packed his manuscripts as a surprise so that he could work on them during their holidays in the mountains. The loss figures in Hemingway's posthumously published memoirs, *A Moveable Feast* (1964), and novel, *The Garden of Eden* (1986). For fictional treatments of the loss, see Joe Haldeman, *The Hemingway Hoax* (New York: Avon Books, 1990), MacDonald Harris, *Hemingway's Suitcase* (New York: Simon and Schuster, 1990), and Nicholas Delbanco, *The Lost Suitcase: Reflections on the Literary Life* (New York: Columbia University Press, 2000).

2. Sandra Whipple Spanier, *Kay Boyle: Artist and Activist* (Carbondale: Southern Illinois University Press, 1986; New York: Paragon House, 1988); *Life Being the Best and Other Stories by Kay Boyle,* ed. Sandra Whipple Spanier (New York: New Directions, 1988).

3. Robert McAlmon, *Being Geniuses Together, 1920-1930,* rev., with supplementary chapters and an afterword by Kay Boyle (Garden City, N.Y.: Doubleday, 1968; rpt., Baltimore: Johns Hopkins University Press, 1997), 68. Subsequent references to this work, abbreviated *BGT,* will appear in the text. In the decade after Robert McAlmon died in obscurity in Arizona in 1956, Boyle resurrected his 1938 memoirs of the expatriate twenties, interleaving her own account in alternating chapters in an unusual dual autobiography that retains McAlmon's original title.

4. See Studs Terkel interview, Apr. 26, 1986, with Kelley Baker, in the Kay Boyle issue of *Twentieth Century Literature* 34.3 (Fall 1988): 304-9, guest edited by Sandra Whipple Spanier.

5. "Kay Boyle," in *Contemporary Authors Autobiography Series* (Detroit: Gale Research Press, 1984), 1:101.

6. Ibid., 1:111.

7. Ibid.

8. Katherine Evans Boyle to Alfred Stieglitz, Jan. 4, 1915, folder 140, box 6, Alfred Stieglitz/Georgia O'Keeffe Archive, Beinecke Rare Book and Manuscript Library, Yale University Library, New Haven, Conn. Issue 47 of *Camera Work,* dated July 1914 but not published until January 1915, includes responses by sixty-eight contributors to the question "What does '291' mean?". Katherine Evans Boyle's is not among them.

9. "Kay Boyle," 1:114.

10. The notebook of poems is in the Kay Boyle Papers, Special Collections, Morris Li-

brary, Southern Illinois University at Carbondale, the primary repository of her unpublished work.

11. Kay Boyle to Joan Boyle, Nov. 9, 1921, folder 12, box 9, Kay Boyle Papers.
12. Ibid.
13. Kay Boyle to Joan Boyle, Dec. 12, 1921, folder 12, box 9, Kay Boyle Papers.
14. Boyle quoted in Harry R. Warfel, *American Novelists of Today* (New York: American Book Company, 1951), 44.
15. On January 4, 1949, the Associated Press reported that "Dr. Lewis Browne, 52, noted rabbi, author and lecturer, who attended the University of Cincinnati, Hebrew Union College and the Rabbinical Seminary was found dead of poisoning, apparently self-administered, yesterday at a Los Angeles Club." Clipping in Browne, Dr. Lewis file, Cincinnati Historical Society.
16. Manifesto, "The Revolution of the Word," *transition* 16-17 (June 1929): 13.
17. Kay Boyle to Doug Palmer, Oct. 24, 1974, Rare Books and Manuscripts Division, Special Collections Library, Pennsylvania State University Libraries, University Park.
18. Margaret Atwood, introduction to Kay Boyle's *Three Short Novels* (New York: Penguin Books, 1982), ix.
19. For a full discussion of the originality of Boyle's narrative methods, see Marilyn Elkins, *Metamorphosizing the Novel: Kay Boyle's Narrative Innovations* (New York: Peter Lang, 1993).
20. Kay Boyle to Lola Ridge, Jan. 26, 1923. The letters from Kay Boyle to Lola Ridge as well as Ridge's correspondence with the Garland Fund administrators are among the holdings of Elaine Sproat, literary executor to Lola Ridge.
21. Leo Litwak, "Kay Boyle—Paris Wasn't Like That," *New York Times Book Review*, July 15, 1984, 1, 32-33.
22. D. A. Callard, *Pretty Good for a Woman: The Enigmas of Evelyn Scott* (London: Jonathan Cape, 1985), 116. See also Mary Wheeling White, *Fighting the Current: The Life and Work of Evelyn Scott* (Baton Rouge: Louisiana State University Press, 1998).
23. Kay Boyle to Katherine Evans Boyle, Aug. 21, 1923, folder 17, box 5, Kay Boyle Papers.
24. Kay Boyle to Katherine Evans Boyle, Oct. 23, 1923, folder 17, box 5, Kay Boyle Papers.
25. Kay Boyle to Joan Boyle, Nov. 21, 1923, folder 12, box 9, Kay Boyle Papers.
26. Evelyn Scott to Lola Ridge, Beziers, France, n.d., letter 150, "Undated letters 2" folder, box 9, Lola Ridge Papers, Sophia Smith Collection, Smith College, Northampton, Mass.
27. An uncle of Albert and Charles Boni, Seltzer had assisted them in establishing Boni and Liveright's Modern Library series in 1918 before leaving the partnership to publish under his own imprint.
28. Kay Boyle to Louise Morgan Theis, July 11, 1925, and Oct. 20, 1925, both in folder 1, Boyle Letters to Louise Morgan Theis, Berg Collection of English and American Literature, New York Public Library, Astor, Lenox, and Tilden Foundations. In her letter to Ridge of December 15, 1924, Boyle had reported that her second book, which would become *Plagued by the Nightingale,* already was "more than begun."
29. William Carlos Williams, "The Somnambulists," *transition* 18 (Nov. 1929), rpt. in *Twentieth Century Literature* 34.3 (Fall 1988): 313-17.

30. Evelyn Scott to Waldo Frank, Dec. 21, 1931, Evelyn Scott folder, box 20, Waldo Frank Papers, Rare Book and Manuscript Library, University of Pennsylvania, Philadelphia.
31. "Kay Boyle," 97.
32. I am grateful to Suzanne Clark for this insight as well as for her groundbreaking contributions to the study of modernism and gender: *Sentimental Modernism: Women Writers and the Revolution of the Word* (Bloomington: Indiana University Press, 1991) and *Cold Warriors: Manliness on Trial in the Rhetoric of the West* (Carbondale: Southern Illinois University Press, 2000).
33. Katherine Anne Porter, "Kay Boyle: Example to the Young," *New Republic* (Apr. 22, 1931), rpt. in *Twentieth Century Literature* 34.3 (Fall 1988): 318.
34. Kay Boyle interviewed in Charles F. Madden, ed., *Talks with Authors* (Carbondale: Southern Illinois University Press, 1968), 231.
35. Kay Boyle to Sandra Spanier, July 17, 1981, collection of Sandra Spanier.

A NOTE ON THE TEXT

The text of this edition of Kay Boyle's *Process* was transcribed from the 119-page carbon typescript in the Berg Collection of English and American Literature at the New York Public Library. I have silently corrected obvious typographical errors, misspellings, and punctuation and have regularized the use of hyphens. I have retained Boyle's capitalization style. I have let stand British spellings (such as *mould, kerb, glamourous*) and have not italicized the French words sprinkled into the sentences in the interest of retaining the original flavor of this manuscript written by an American abroad. I have not tampered with Boyle's syntax or word choice in the spirit of the manifesto to which she put her name in 1929. According to the manifesto that called for the "Revolution of the Word": "The literary creator has the right to disintegrate the primal matter of words imposed on him by text-books and dictionaries," and "He has the right to use words of his own fashioning and to disregard existing grammatical and syntactical laws."

process

1 In four directions from a bronze fountain, Cincinnati, Ohio.* Streets curl into the hills and wired inclines above them stand sharp like long-legged birds in fume. The hills lean away from the smoke, lean away from the river that cleaves them.

Kerith Day made a song against the city, shouting it as she drove above the river. The motor sang with her, jerked words into air that was heavy and shaped with smoke. In the rear seat a woman moved against the singing.

"Your voice is dreadful." And she added: "But I don't want you to stop." Slender, in blue, her hands moving in her lap on the wakeful Pekinese. Her fingers in unreleased movement over their stiff copper hair.

Kerith felt her words and her quick motion, sounds more purposeful than meaning, singing again as a man on a motor-wheel passed them. His hair blew back in the wind and he lifted one hand to them, smiling.

The woman leaned outward on her elbow to follow the unbroken curve of his progress. "Who was that?"

"I don't know. Youth escaping. Isn't he nice." Kerith's face in the windshield fluttered heavy above thin shoulders, dark thick hair cut

---

* The Tyler Davidson Memorial Fountain, given to the city by Henry Probasco in 1871 in memory of his late brother-in-law, is a Cincinnati landmark. The *Genius of Water* portrays a female figure with outstretched arms from whose fingers water falls onto sculpted figures facing outward in four directions. Throughout, the novel is true to Cincinnati landmarks and geography, from the descriptions of Eden Park to the ferry that ran to the amusement park at Coney Island to the inclined planes that were constructed in the late nineteenth century to transport streetcars and enable the city set in a basin on the Ohio River to expand into the surrounding hills.

short in her neck, nose and brow high and large. There was no invulnerable beauty under the long strong line of her brows. Behind her the woman cried: "Oh, the sky! Do you see the sky! Oh, isn't it lovely! Oh, do let's stop here for one cigaret!"

Grass unraveled stiffly to the bank, dark opulent earth flung precipitant upon the long low rails, where freight cars side-tracked by the river widened the soiled short houses of factory workers.

The woman gave Kerith a cigaret, leaning to her until her hat brim touched Kerith's hair. Her hand on the seat-back turned restive and Kerith relaxed into motion, bowing her head down to the woman's hand.

She moved her hand under Kerith's kiss looking away with the blur of smoke. "If I'd always had someone to be a part—going on easily and stopping simply when one felt like stopping. I never really wanted anything more." Her wanting had no identity. Kerith felt her analyzing the voids of an abstract woman. "Uncle Peter liked stopping this way over the river. One night—did I tell you—a machine flashed its lights on us and he covered his face with his hat."

Kerith turned from her exposed and inexplicable to him, but the woman proceeded gently: "He felt that because he was a well-known business-man it wouldn't do for him to be seen stopping in the park that way. But I couldn't, I just couldn't ever feel the same about him. It made so much difference."

The river sucked at the flat dull breast of Kentucky.

"It wouldn't matter what experiences he could have," said the woman. "His instincts were too wrong." She was sure of her emotion. "Experiences can't be fundamental. People go on untouched."

"You have." Kerith groped suddenly for words. "Thinking that if you can simply *tell* people they're bound to understand. And they never do. You realize that and yet you go on." She felt bitterly like her father, smiling sheepishly over words. "Dad. I can't. No amount of telling him will ever make him see me. We never happened to each other."

They sat soundless, incurious, until the woman said: "And I've thought so often what a very little change in his attitude would mean. If he only tried to reach you on some definite basis . . ."

Kerith blew thin menacing smoke at her reflection. "Oh, what's the use . . ."

The woman cried out: "But there is use in recognizing possibilities! I don't want you wasted here with them and what they can offer you. I want you away from here. I don't want little things absorbing you . . ."

Her hand turned softly in Kerith's neck, voice gravely caressing. "There is so much ahead of you."

Her voice swayed the ripe phase of Kerith's life. Work in her father's office was without finality. It was his unending existence, but for her it ripened, it had grown heavy and was ready to drop away from her.

The woman threw her cigaret stub through the window.

"The pink's all gone. Shall we move along?"

Square-bottomed boats opened light on the river, squatted above with their lights long sallow claws spread in the dark flesh of water. The car above followed the road curve. A distant arch held factory roofs and a few high lights, stiff and thin.

"Can you see it?" Kerith's voice peered into the lights.

"No-oo-oo." She strained on Kerith's shoulder.

"Yes. There. See." Kerith lifted one hand from the wheel, pointing.

Through the arch and below them, electric letters "JESSE DAY AND SON, Drive In" flashed back into the roofs, grew up gradually again, erect and frail.

"God," said the woman. "They've got courage."

Kerith sickened with the emotion.

"Oh, *please.*"

A slow dark smear spread on the road, thick heaviness sounding the luminous white.

"Oh, it needed that" laughed Kerith. "Red paint enormously spilled. Like blood. Pervading shadow. Isn't it nice."

By the arch in a dark spume of figures a broken motorcycle burned crisply. Kerith flashed to knowledge. A man turned from the group, eager, smiling. "They took him to the hospital, but he was dead all right. Car threw him right through the arch and broke his neck."

The women moaned against each other, strange sound to the Pekinese who pressed at the window crying sharply at the blaze.

Kerith accepted dark streets, rocking slowly through them as though in grief. Factories were closed as they passed them, walls sagging spent from the taut window-frames. Kerith saw them, factories conceived before the perfect machine erection, enduring unborn, aborted from the age-womb and transfused with life of the workers. They were old and tedious, but the cost would be too tremendous should they be done away with and re-created in the perfect machine conception. They stood potent with deep obscene being.

The shop wallowed between them, low and wide under its crown of white letters. Kerith drove through the garage entrance, at one end a flight of stairs and at the top a glass door with light yellowing through it, upon it "OFFICE" in unyielding black. Kerith stepped on the stone floor. "Blood on the tire." She leaned to the wheel. He was tied by these things. He was tied by the voices of men in the park talking of him. Kerith felt the other woman near in the darkness and put her arms about her.

"Mother," she said, "let's let him go. We won't tell them, will we?"

The women were one, rooted together in darkness. Kerith knew her mother's face unprotected below her, the lifted given emotion of her face. She looked down into darkness, but from this knowledge there was no immunity.

A man opened the high door, standing small and hesitant at the head of the steps. "What's up?" Kerith's father stood with one hand on the knob, hesitant. The half-opened door channeled light on the two women. Separately they moved to the stairs.

"There was a man killed in the park." Light betrayed them.

"What," he remarked loudly. "What."

They followed each other, climbing the long flight to him.

"Where. Where did you say!"

"By the arch."

The office withdrew from light. They came through, into the passage and the large dim library beyond. A bald stooped little man hurried out, drying his hands in a towel. The Pekinese stood off barking sharply at the strange white towel swinging toward them.

"What is it, Harry?" He vindicated himself behind his brows.

"There was someone killed." Kerith's father was useless in his lack of knowledge of the thing. His eyes protruded into the backs of his wife and daughter as they crossed the room.

"Someone killed?" Wind blustered his mustache. "For God's sake why doesn't someone answer me?"

"Yes, someone killed by the arch."

His son had no more words. Kerith felt desiccation within her, but her mother turned at the door, saying brightly: "We don't know any more than you, daddy. We just got there and saw the motorcycle burning by the arch."

"What arch, Nora?" The old man pronounced each sound low and singly as though he spoke to a child. "What arch? Why don't you explain?"

The woman came into Kerith's bedroom, away from the suspended men.

"What in the name of God is the matter with them?" the old man whispered fiercely. He felt their lives closing against him, silences holding up to him that he was contemptibly responsible for their present, and he would not oppose them. He had been fine and immaculate too, and now he could dust his office, empty waste-baskets with his fine small hands, believing his own words that nothing was menial. He could have tolerated anything from them other than this hard free dependence on each other which so definitely excluded him.

He followed his son from the room with quick forward little steps.

"Why don't they answer me?" he thrust into his son's silence.

Harry Day hesitated at the door, his shoulders thin under the tired folds of his coat. The will of the other man was forcing him out. His father moved toward him.

"Oh, no, don't go, don't go."

"Oh, I think I'll have a look."

The door closed tentatively and the old man stepped down after a moment and pushed it firmly into place. He saw his son crossing the street-light with his bright uncertain walk. Somewhere he knew him as a part of his own will protruded into the night, but his mind was solicitous and unrevealed, caring about his son.

He returned, short slow steps, to the wash-room, hearing through the maché partition motion of voices of the two in Kerith's room.

2 The shop was low in the street, wide windows opened and veined with electric wires. Heat rolling up with the dust fell on the naked floor, full and unspent. Windows sucked heat in their white cheeks. The switchboard broke out with its hard nasal little voice. Kerith swung in her chair to the black mouth on which clung drops of dew-like heat. The old man came from his office, drawing her close under his brows.

"Shall I have Al bring you an electric fan?"

He creaked away from her voice, back into the little office that was his bedroom as well. He was sagged and heavy with heat, his stomach leading forward, his short arms fallen in the sleeves of his alpaca coat.

The door from the shop opened before Nora, with her a tall leaning woman whose throat widened up cool to her smooth-lying hair.

"Come in when you can for a drink."

Nora followed Rebekah through the screen swing-door of the passage, thrusting herself thinly up, loving Rebekah as she loved Matzenhauer,* the immutable throated column that was the great source of perfect strength. Nora would turn to Kerith at a concert: "Her arms like *eight* of ours," stemming erect in the coat that dragged at her shoulders.

When Kerith could come into them Nora lay on the lounge smoking, living wholly in the brandished voice of the other woman.

"If I go on diluting myself, where shall I be?"

Nora nodded, deliberate and slow.

---

* Margaret Matzenhauer was a renowned contralto.

"I think it fine that you see directly what you must do with your life. No false sentiment."

Nora clung to this singleness in Rebekah, but for her it was without beauty. If she could so reduce herself there would be no stimulus nor conception in life. But as an ultimate phase she wanted this completion, to become in her person irreducible, and then to be dead.

Dust lay finely wrinkled on the table. A sharp edge of light cut the down-drawn blind and a metal bowl on the sill reflected and projected concave brilliance. The room shrunk to shallow darkness, the kitchen door open on a glass table top and shelves pompous with light.

"I shall withdraw from everything that does not bear directly on my law study," said Rebekah.

About them the mind of Nora was pure and warm with love, her perfect love for their individual directions. Kerith sat near, touching Rebekah's dress, fingers resting in the good-smelling cloth.

"Concentration will mean solid colors?"

The stiffish brown stuff with its shell-shaped coral pattern fell crevassed below her fingers. Rebekah's eyes smiled.

"Brodsky says black and white. White stockings and low-heeled slippers so that my feet will be like music notes."

Slowly a smile rumbled up in her.

"Max . . ." Smile prolonging her husband's name, ". . . abhors Brodsky. He thinks his body is so repulsive."

Her words were like a wound in Nora. Rebekah dulled the tip of her cigaret, spoke with a slow pointed revealing.

"It is true that Brodsky, that Brodsky stresses his body."

"But to me," said Nora quickly and softly, "his way of dressing is not an emphasis, no, it is not an emphasis. It becomes a part of him."

Rebekah stirred under the unbearable purity of Nora's voice.

"But in other ways."

She lifted her cup, talking through the blurred edge, and Kerith went to Nora and lay with her on the lounge. Nora was destroyed, her fingers living in Kerith's hair. "Relationships are so rarely complete, rarely."

Nora spoke with a slow pain between her eyes, and Kerith leaned into her voice, the deft flowing movement of her mouth, putting her body against Nora as though to staunch her. She felt Nora unborn, her skin and flesh delicate and unborn. She was like taut quick flesh about the body of Nora.

The unreleased following of fingers stirred in Kerith's hair, and Nora turned finally to laughter.

"That's why I'm glad that I'm not young and beautiful. Youth and beauty! Brodsky can come directly to me without prejudice. In you and Kerith there is mystery."

Nora was no older than Rebekah but her body was thin and fallen. Rebekah's hands were unfrayed and her flesh bridled unbroken. Her voice smouldered in her throat.

"Yes, there's mystery in you. It's the human offering that we understand. The sacrifice wholly consumed, never a part withdrawn. That we understand. It sprang from us. It's mystery because we can no longer believe. It has gone from us. It withered in us."

"But it's in you, it's in you," cried Nora gently, her long cheeks flushed with emotion. "The perfect form of it is in you. Strong action flowing from the source of life. That is the perfect form of it."

Rebekah refused this, shaking her head. But Nora would not believe, would never believe them so separate. They were silent, ebbing to each other in an inscrutable astral urge, Rebekah in denial and Nora in knowing the sub-flame emotion in Rebekah that could finally live and fuse them.

As they sat poised, Rebekah's child came up from their car, solid steps across the hall. Her body pressed up from brown downed knees into her full sashed belly. She leaned on Rebekah, swinging her heavy droop of hair in her neck.

Kerith went from their voices into the office, to heat dropped like an unstirred curtain.

From the street door the dark arched eyes of a man lifted.

"Is there any sort of vacancy here?"

Kerith clenched in his voice.

"I'm sorry. There's nothing."

His hand fell back on the door. The old man pattered from his office and stood looking down the steps.

"What is it, sir?"

"I wanted work"

The old man fingered his pocket.

"I'm afraid there's nothing here, my man."

He followed down, leaning back from the drag of his belly.

"Here's something to tide you over." The old man reached from his pocket. He came up pleasantly, dusting his palms.

"A case to which the strikers may point with pride."

Twang of the switchboard hummed the heat.

3 Labor Temple is an orange barn shuffled between tenements. Kerith waited in the Ford, past the Ohio Mechanics Institute where for three years she had studied. She had known well the sons of men who now talked in Labor Temple, had been part of the freed unfearing mass of youth, stirring to purpose. They had known their own strength—sun dripped over their long blonde arms, bread-white legs stretched in motion in the fog-water of the Ohio River—youth, growing to the fear of its own strength. Separately they had accepted the purpose of age and the created truth of unenduring freedom. The mass disintegrated, coming to the direction of age as the direction of progress.

And now beyond them youth was accepting the truth of its own being. In Germany, in Austria there was the movement of youth. Nowhere else was there a turning from the streets to the cool flesh of grass under naked feet. Youth turning from the cities, without sentiment, without glorification of the act, simply the quiet acknowledgment and use of what they found most unopposed about them. The purism of youth, untouched by sentiment or belief, accepting what was beyond the cities as least symphonic with the life they had chosen not to lead.

Walnut Street is soiled and broken, cobbles spat roughly apart. Over them a man came stepping quickly between mud runnels, his shoulders drawn smally in, head drawn in, holding every part of his narrowed. His arms and legs escaped, moving loose and long. He watched the cobbles for gaps, jumping aside to evade the mud. It was Soupault, who came facing Kerith, his lean wolfish smile over his French handshake high and wristless.

"It is pleasing to have a car."

His fingers spread on the door with thumb heads flaring up wide. He was fragile beneath his loud tossed English, his wrists lean-fibered dark and silky. Hot light through the glass blinded his bright bare face.

"That is Labor Temple," said Kerith.

He looked over his shoulder and the muscle strained down into his collar. His fingertips pressed back on the door turned white with dull dark moons rising beneath the nail.

"Oh, that is Labor Temple."

There were great black and red-lettered posters by the door. Russia—speakers, William Z. Foster and Lincoln Steffens.* His face came back to her smiling.

"You are with the workers?"

"With the radicals."

"And in America the radicals and the workers are not one thing?"

It amused him.

"Oh, no. They're largely opposed. The workers opposed to the radicals."

His shoulders shrugged under the sudden snap of his mouth. He was strange to Kerith. Her mind moved curiously in him. He laughed, drawn lean and fine.

"Well, I can't bother. I'm the French army."

Today he was narrowed in brown.

"I liked your uniform," said Kerith.

"But not what it means." Soupault stood with eyes turned pure and amused.

She felt his mind alert and amused behind his opaque eyes. His fingers tapped lightly and rapidly at the top of the door, profile standing up in light, his eyes turned away and reading the posters.

Men emerged in groups talking, and Nora came down from them, carrying full nodding boughs of whelk. The leaves were a cool

---

* William Z. Foster (1881–1961) was a leader in the American Federation of Labor during the 1919 steel strike. In 1921 he became one of the top Communist party leaders in the United States, running for president in 1924, 1928, and 1932. Lincoln Steffens (1866–1936), a "muckraking" journalist, the editor of *McClure's* magazine, and a political philosopher sympathetic to many Communist aims but unaffiliated with the party, lectured widely in the United States, promoting social and political reform.

shower on her throat. Soupault stood back timid and angular before her approach.

"Aren't they lovely, lovely!" she cried.

Petal leaves pressed on the glass and the flowers of the bush hung sullen, the boughs broken off in smooth white wounds. Nora's face hung above, soft and compassionate.

"The Sacco and Vanzetti protest meeting is tonight, at the shop."* She spoke to Soupault. "Will you come . . . you will come."

When they had driven from him Kerith's mind cleared to an aloof pause in which to isolate and remember him. The bone bareness of his face and dark hands, invulnerable bareness broken to the deep suck of his eyes. And in them there was an impending beauty, an imminent life and sign.

At night Rebekah and Brodsky were the first to come, and a stranger who would not be drawn in with them, sat pressing Nee Nee's paws down from his knee with the folded staff of his newspaper. Brodsky stood with Kerith, his flesh white in the neck of his black smock and his palms pressing broad on his hips.

"The light across the corner . . . like a shadow of light . . . light dimensional and casting a pure shadow, isn't it?"

His voice drew her softly in him, excluding the room. She felt herself drawn into his cool remote being, away from the confusion of the room.

After the speaker had done, Nora searched for pencils, switched on the light in her bedroom beyond, searching on the heavy top of the dark chest. The edge of green almond-faced tapestry fell above the drawer-knobs. Two men who sat near the door turned to each other and one lifted his shoulder to the new room. Kerith came to their voices below her.

". . . for a radical meeting, the elegant office of a boss, with Turkey rugs and swell dogs. You bet we wouldn't be in their home, oh, even if we have got the same politics . . ."

Kerith went with Nora to gather in the names and addresses.

---

* The case of Nicola Sacco and Bartolomeo Vanzetti, Italian anarchists accused of two murders that had taken place in Boston in April 1920, became a cause célèbre among many artists and intellectuals, who felt they were on trial for their radical politics as much as for any crime. They were convicted on July 14, 1921, in the Massachusetts Superior Court before Judge Webster Thayer. Maintaining their innocence to the end and despite widespread protests in their support, they were executed on August 23, 1927.

"The men near the door think this is dad's office."

Nora smiled dazzled and uncomprehending. Kerith thought of the room bare, chairs and no hangings at the windows. *That* the men could have accepted without confusion, and if the perfect accord were wanted then everything must go down in clearance for it. But she could not believe in any final accord, not between Nora and the workers, not between any aware beings.

"Why don't you tell them we live here?" she said.

Nora crossed to the doorway, came to them, unprotected.

"Of course, you understand, you know of course that this is our home." Her voice was soft and exposed to them. "This is where we live, my daughter, Mr. Day, and his father. This is our living room."

The man who had spoken saw the rugs, the pure lemon lamp, long soft chairs and lounge, the walls cleared to reproductions of Brancusi brasses. He sat pumping his thumbs into the blue velvet chair, seeing the room.

"But it doesn't seem these things goes with the labor movement."

"Yes, oh, yes, why not?" Nora's voice stemmed eager and full.

His voice drifted up to her. "These pictures here. They don't mean anything to us."

"Yes, oh, yes!" cried Nora. "You're wrong. That's just what's wrong everywhere. Everyone concentrated, concentrated, and that's where the change has got to come. You haven't time for art and the artists are concentrated in themselves. That's where the change must come." Nora turned eagerly to the wall, lifting down the framed white oblong. "This is a photograph of the work of Brancusi. Brancusi, an individual, and he and the labor movement are deeply, deeply united. He produces this and there are people just as ready to call him a criminal as there are people to cry out on a Lenin or any of your radical thinkers."

The man held the sheer and light-blotted picture. Brodsky who stood behind him in the passage spoke softly.

"They can't be taught that."

But Kerith saw Nora close only to her own sharp reaction to the man and her belief in him. He sat looking down upon the brass sitting figure with its hard lovely up-drawn legs.

"They get satisfaction somewheres from working like that. That's the difference. We work to keep alive. I guess that's where the difference comes in."

The other worker leaned to the picture, thick eyeglasses touching the frame, bringing his voice to words. His head beat with the jut of his voice.

"They know, they know. They can say what it's like. They see a sun going down, and they can say what it's like."

His head beat with his words, beat in his silence.

"But it's better to feel that, than to say it in any way. The feeling of it is what matters."

His head beat with Nora's voice, beat unbelieving. Brodsky too withdrew from Nora's mind. If he believed this the structure of life would collapse. He accepted knowledge as the one individual solution, blunting the sharp denying ecstasy of his perceptions. His heart turned questioning, but his mind would have absolute knowledge surrendered. He acquiesced in the university violation, fearing the deception of any other way of learning.

Soupault came quietly out of the dark hall, unperceived, and moved sharply away from them as though aware of being moulded to their words behind the workers. Nora had left a silence in which he exchanged tobacco with the two men. But he was separate from the workers, in fear. He forced smiling to efface in him that which they saw. Words slipped uneasily between.

When the numberless people broke slowly out, he walked alone down the timber steps. Rebekah and Brodsky lingered, and Kerith in the kitchen made coffee, waiting the sullen plurp in the percolator. Brodsky came massively in to her, limping with his rheumatism, stood close and silent, white-fleshed beside her. Kerith felt him close and womanly, his hands lifting the date box, fingers delicately and heavily parting the lips of oiled paper at the mouth. He selected delicate bits of the glaucous meat, spacing them upon the platter.

They sat drinking as the old man and his son came in from the movies. Harry Day was diminished in guilt, smiling, and the old man sat with them, eating perfectly a piece of coffee cake. H. D. effaced himself, taking the dogs out in the lot. The old man became charming and gallant in his response to Nora, creating a passive world in the action of their voices. He spoke lightly, in poised compassion. "And the meeting was all that it should have been?"

Nora winged utterly to him, nodding.

"Collection telegraphed to Boston. There were over sixty here. It was all alive, all keenly alive."

"Ah, that was a good showing indeed!"

Nora turned the pamphlets on the table.

"These are the little books we passed out, giving the case impartially."

The old man felt for his glasses, dropping crumbs from his fingertips.

"There's little in the papers," he said pleasantly. "I should be interested in knowing the facts."

Rebekah and Kerith were remembering aloud and with laughter:

"'Skiddeth bus and sloppeth us,' and then 'the ague hath my ham,' isn't it?"

"Yes, 'skiddeth bus and sloppeth us, the ague hath my ham, sing God *damn!*'"*

The old man looked up gently. "Oh, Kerith, hush, hush! That isn't a pretty thing you're saying."

He turned a page of the booklet, cleared his throat, speaking mildly: "I note here that the prisoners were tried in a *cage.* I can scarcely credit that statement."

"Oh, a bit of staging," said Brodsky, "to influence public and jury."

"I don't think it possible," said the old man lightly. "It is absolutely against Supreme Court ruling, as you know, Mrs. Woolf." He turned to Rebekah. He too had been a lawyer. "I don't see how such a thing could under any circumstances occur in an United States courtroom."

"But it did happen!" cried Nora, flushed and eager.

The old man cleared his throat gently through Nora's voice from the lounge.

"They were known to be active in radical labor. It was impossible for them to be given an unbiased trial."

---

* These lines are from Ezra Pound's poem "Ancient Music," first published in *Blast* 2 (July 1915).

Behind his eyeglasses the old man was rooted in faith. Nora who knew him now, impervious, destructive, stood clear of him. She had lived with him in torturous self-demolition, subduing her instincts in acknowledgment of his haughty mind. Now she stood free, but her voice reached out to him.

"I don't believe it possible," he repeated lightly.

4 White eyes of the switchboard lolled upon the heat. A cool-beaked wind pecked at Kerith's throat, drooped away as though suddenly oppressed by the weight of heat.

Before evening Kerith and Brodsky drove into the hills and wandered down though unreaped grass, turning in their contentment to see the grass restored over their steps to its raw strong unbroken flow. Trees gnarled dark arms above the wheat. Daisies followed in the glamourous descent of crystal stalks, swinging surfeited with rich warm petals dripping from their mouths.

The forest fell like a shadow discoloring the hill. Sensitive, antennae-like the first trees advanced into the spume of wheat. The feet of the two walking scarred moss that glided from them smoothly into the stark bone agony of brush. The cry of an axe singing down through timber cleared space in which a cabin staggered against trees.

Facing the dark odor and gloom of the door, a negro bowed with the axe, releasing great clumps of sweet wood from the bark.* Pearls of sweat lifted in his ribs. Chickens scattered in the path and Brodsky stopped engrossed in the unripe fowl whose coarse shrewd feet spatulated among grain. The negro's body rounded to face them.

"You couldn't let us have a chicken, could you?"

Brodsky's smile dodged the light that filled his nose-glasses. The negro came down, crouched, and with a quick wide gesture flecked up the body of a pullet. The bird's tail reared empty below his lurch-

---

* Capitalization of *Negro* was irregular before 1930, when the *New York Times* announced in a March 7 editorial that it henceforth would capitalize the word. It appears lowercase in Boyle's typescript.

ing neck, yellow claws clutched and shriveled light. The negro stood ruminant, nipples ringed vibrant and blue as fungus.

"Not enough meat to bother."

The fowl, released, flew sharply toward the house and the negro stood rooted before them, boughs hanging heavy. He looked softly up to them.

"Spuds I *can* offer you. Any number."

"Oh, it would be nice to have some!" cried Brodsky. "Roasted."

The clear firm body of the negro moved away to the cabin, and they waited, turning from the sour odor of chickens. His hands served them but his body was suspended. His back flowed into dark patterns of thew, tapering to raw stabs of light. Kerith felt the white stretch of her skin like a sterility upon her. She watched his unconscious descent with the paper of potatoes, and his fingers subtle and alert following them into Brodsky's sack.

"Well, how much will it be?" Brodsky was at ease between them.

The negro wiped his palms in his skirt, humming his voice.

"Would you try my liquor? That's all . . . if you'd try my liquor."

Brodsky moved smiling, affable in protest, and the negro returned to them with a brown-paunched jug and a terrier bitch who followed in abasement, cringing forward on her thick slack hams, trailing her wet abased emotion. The negro poured them liquor and his mouth closed over the jug, lips webbed like old palms and edged pink as the lifted cushion of his palm. His throat straightened down wide again.

Kerith drank and spat out, holding her throat. Laughter sang up in the negro gently.

"Goes down easier a second time, yo find."

They sat drinking, Brodsky speaking with the negro, and Kerith wondering over the reverberations which widened from the clear core of his acceptance of them.

"You live alone," she said presently, without question.

"Yes . . . I live alone . . . I stay clear away from town."

The slow hum of his voice between them.

"You *are* free, aren't you?" Kerith thrust grave inquiry from under her brows. Brodsky startled the sharp drink full into his throat.

The negro looked gently at Kerith, unstirred, sounding her word in the rhythm of his mouth.

"Free . . . free . . . well, I've got taxes to pay." He looked away to the apple-green fume of the forest. "Just like the rest of them. I pays my taxes."

As he spoke his eyes in their firm albescent globes moved slowly against light. Kerith followed their movement to the cabin where the full rick leaned with barley, and gourds ripening against the dipping step were flushing a slow deep gold from green. Melons of globular light flanked the reposed angles of his cow. Her under-lip was a bright moist line shifting rhythmically above the rich and bitter straw.

Kerith leaned her elbows on her knees, looking to the dark sweet flesh of the negro. His eyes paused upon her, and then he turned. His voice, excluding her from the voluptuous harvest, hummed. "It is best in winter. The snow comes and there are just my footmarks in it."

"Ah, yes," said Kerith, vibrant. His eyes lifted, open to her, approached and almost included her, and then closed back into his unshaken soul.

Brodsky was degraded when he saw Kerith thus, renouncing all truth of her own being and accepting to the depths of her the life of another.

"Yes, it must be a relief not to see people," he said brightly. "But if you are really liberated in yourself, they can't matter. I feel perfectly able to be with people, any people, as long as I *know* I am free in myself."

"Oh, you do, do you?" said Kerith. She wanted to feel her body lean and sharp in freedom.

"I don't believe there can be any real, any material freedom," said Brodsky. "Somewhere we all have to conform. But if your mind is your own, you're all right, it seems to me."

The negro listened to Brodsky, wiping his mouth over the back of his hand. Brodsky's cool white voice drew an impeccable line between mind and body. To be away from the precise insistence of his voice rose in Kerith as an approach to a corporeal freedom. She leapt up, gesturing her inward impatience, and left Brodsky to a solitary betrayal of the negro.

She walked away from them, down to the streaming water. The evening of pure blue glass splintered on flame, and the stream gully writhed barren of trees, dark vein of water bearing a scar of flame.

Kerith's feet were blue-lipped under water, her gathered skirts bruised on her knees. White water spouted from her ankles. The stones were cold flesh on the palms of her feet.

Kerith felt the cold full touch of water and stone, the dark bushes against her like puffs of wind, restoring silence in her. She walked wonderingly up the land, watching the sky burn and pale to wax. She moved in the clear spaces between the firm-breasted bush feeling the miracle of restored silence in her. Presently wondering white lights of worms tingled out near the water, and below in the taper of the stream, river-birches were black and semen-podded against the clear pure wave of sky.

She walked slowly up, feeling herself in movement in the perfect unfecundated womb.

At the hill-crest bushes withdrew from her body. There was a prescient stir, a fore-knowledge of sound, and Kerith paused in herself awaiting its final emersion from silence. Land crouched in the gully, tightening dry fingers in the stream-throat, and the unstuck protest of water hung imminent, its full hollow warble fore-sounding in Kerith.

She stood long under the deepening flow of darkness, and then came the outer violation, the far threshing down in the brush beyond the water and the flicker of flame. Tree stems struck clear against the spreading stain of fire, dark slender stalks balding the flesh of the forest. She waited until light was withdrawn again to the solid flag of flame, and then she made the long descent slowly, odors new in her nostrils, senses vulnerable, as though regiven to life. She came silently into the fire-ring and stood drying her feet in light.

Brodsky crouched over the little gunny-sack, poking potatoes into the ash. He moved away, in absorption, seeking branches for the sausage-roasting, and stood in light whitening the long boughs to points. Kerith lay in the fire-ring listening to the life-movement of the forest, the dry canny throttling of a tree-toad and cricket voices that pricked warily tentatively into darkness. Senses were erect in her and miraculously exposed, as though the husk of being had withered from her. She felt that to remain thus was the logical and simple acceptance of life, and that the return to any other way of living was a conscious perversion.

"I like you as issue from the loins of Wotan,"* said Brodsky across flame.

He worked under the feather of smoke.

"The conclusion escapes us," said Kerith stretching. "You couldn't possibly come through."

"Do you know, I think I could." He looked up.

"No," said Kerith. "Whatever there is to you would be consumed in flame. By the time you got to the other side, you would no longer exist. Your lovely draperies would go up—pouf! Your luscious jewels turned over and over on the ravished tongues . . ."

Brodsky sat back on his heels, smiling between his cheeks.

"But if there was, beneath everything, a clear separate core of which you know nothing, nothing at all—"

"There isn't," said Kerith.

"You've only one more year to talk that way," said Brodsky. "One can't be arrogant and charming after twenty."

Kerith stretched thin and angular fingers to the flame. She pointed out to the water that streamed beyond their charmed ring, dark inscrutable coil of progress.

"Civilization lies at the source, where the water is almost stagnant. Only one vein flows now. It is part of me. I love it. I love the fullness that it can come to."

"Why metaphoric?" said Brodsky. "Why metaphysics?" He shook his head. "And lots better 'the fullness to which it can come.'"

"Ah, well, perhaps it would be," said Kerith. "But at least it's only the sound cores of being that can float down the stream."

"I'm not sure I want to float away," said Brodsky. "Perhaps I'd rather stagnate. I'm not sure I want to leave civilization."

He worked silent awhile, engrossed with the splitting of the meat.

"Do you really think you *could?*" he said finally. "Do you feel you could simply let go of everything?"

"Yes," said Kerith. "Humanity to be re-conceived, re-taken into the womb. Even to rot in the womb, rather than be reborn in the old method of life."

---

* Wotan is one of the names of Odin, the Norse god of war, the protector of heroes, and the god of poets.

"Delightful!" said Brodsky. "I *do* know what you mean. The unfertilized corrosion of the womb."

He lifted his head, suddenly stirred.

"Yes, I do know how you feel about humanity, exactly, exactly, but I do think you can come beyond that. I think you *will* come beyond that when you are fully balanced in yourself." He looked up to her, drawn past her in the stir of his belief. "There is a degree of mental knowing that you can come to that surpasses everything. It takes you on in an absolute ecstacy."

Kerith listened to the clear ring of his voice.

"You believe that, don't you?" she said. She wanted to accept this with him, to be submerged in the flow of his belief.

"Oh, I *know*," he cried. "I know there is an impregnable state of mind, a progression of knowledge that is beyond anything." He swayed with the stress of his rising emotion. "You remember Ducasse's created aura, you remember 'one moment you appeared to my enchanted view clad in the insignia of youth . . .'"*

"It is very beautiful," said Kerith out of shadow.

Brodsky lifted his face as though to a benediction, repeating the words deeply as they came to him.

"'One moment you appeared to my enchanted view clad in the insignia of youth . . . but I allowed you to drop into chaos like a diving bell . . . you will never emerge . . . it is enough for me that I have your memory . . . you must give place to other substance maybe less beautiful which the stormy overflow of a love . . . resolved not to quench its thirst in the human race . . . will give birth to.'" His hands were fallen heavy and sensitive, twitching on his thick knees. His voice rose swaying. "'Starved love . . . which would devour itself did it not seek its food in celestial images . . . finally creates a pyramid of seraphim more numerous than the insects which swarm a drop of water . . . and will weave them in an ellipse . . . which will whirl about him.'" His voice which had risen to an acute and vibrant pitch, with-

---

* The French poet Isadore-Lucien Ducasse (1846–70), who wrote under the pseudonym Comte de Lautréamont, achieved posthumous popularity among the Surrealists, who considered him an exemplary figure. Selections from his long prose poem, *Les Chants de Maldoror,* translated by John Rodker, were published in installments in *Broom* beginning in the August 1922 issue. Here Brodsky quotes directly from the third and fourth canto of "The Lay of Maldoror" as published in *Broom* 3.4 (Nov. 1922): 286.

drew to the final words, subdued. "'Meanwhile . . . the traveler arrested by the appearance of a cataract . . . could see in the distance . . . did he lift his face . . . a human being led towards the cave of hell . . . by a garland of living camellias . . .'"

Kerith saw him shaken under the full transfigured flow of his voice.

"To live, and to know that, and beyond that!" he cried. "To have sensitive, sensitive resources of knowledge!"

Kerith watched him in depression, dry under the dissolution of his voice. She could never go on with him in this. She saw him clear and unconfused, with his own sacred fire unquenchable in him. But for her it was too complete, it was too perfect. She saw him remote from her, warm-bodied and sure, bending over the fire, his flesh still holding the beatified transfigured glow.

He prodded potatoes from the ashes, his hands still agitated from his emotion, and they ate across flame, the crisp black crust of meat good in their mouths.

It was perilously beautiful when they followed the stream-throat out, walking back in the cool cavernous echo of water. The moonlight was a cold white tide rising, lapping slowly on the tree trunks, hissing under the brush. The Ford huddled like an owl in the roadside.

They descended in a white wake of dust past one-eyed houses that drowsed at their moorings. Midway the hill sagged open on the river, the city like a tarnished frill at the lean crook of its elbow.

They drove down into the outskirts where drugstore windows bleared the corners, and from the intimacies of movie shows oozed a watery discharge of faces. Heat paunched up close at a crossing, jutted in a blue uniform, stopping the Ford with elbows on the window leaning in.

"Never heard of the dimming law, eh?"

Kerith straightened towards him.

"What do you mean?"

He gave her a blue card.

"Tomorrow morning, nine o'clock. What's your name?"

"What have I done?" said Kerith.

"Lights too bright." He stood, kindly, taking her name and address. "The Judge will tell you the rest tomorrow."

Sedately the Ford backed away, swung over the lean river. On Race Street the arcade entrance slit thin-lipped between buildings. Brodsky turned curiously, and Kerith saw him passive in rage, seeking vindication.

"I've never been through in a car," he said. He lifted one indolent hand to the paved arcade.

"No one has."

Kerith turned recklessly into the walk. This to strike as a true assertion of their inviolable being. The wheels butted the kerb. Brodsky flowed in a quick silent flow of energy to the street, pulled at one wheel and lifted with his back. The tire soiled his wide palms. He looked up, crying: "If someone could only get hold of the other side!"

A man stopped curious, watched curiously, and then stepped blankly and eagerly in. The two men shouldered together. The stranger's face lifted, shriveled with his effort. "If I hadn't lost this hand in the war she'd be up in a jiffy. It was the war that done it," he said.

The car swelled forward over them, the front wheels bulging over the kerb. Brodsky came in, dusting his palms, smiling, sat secretly smiling through the arcade, past the windows clean with haberdashery, the shrill insensate fling of cheap jewelry.

They drove slowly, in silent and profound laughter, rocked slowly into Vine Street. Sky in the breach of buildings grew up like a dark firm flower.

5 Blanched blade of light transfixed her in revolving gloom. In the lumber-yard beyond the window shavings were turned on the tongue of the moon to dark voluted foam. Planked timber broke upward in angular gulfs to the sill.

Kerith stepped bare-foot on the white floor. Her body out of the gown swayed between the window and the mirror in supernatural height. There was a glamourous beauty on her flesh as though she had emerged from the slow gulfing sea of the yard. She spread her fingers on her bladed ribs, seeking the movement of the dark impenetrable flow that stirred within her. She knew it, turning against the angles of her body, deeply acknowledged in her. It was this that existed that Brodsky would not admit. She remembered the cool impeccable edge of his voice between body and mind.

In Nora there was recognition, quivering taut in her, acknowledgment of them as separate veins leaping from one source. It was too profound to sheathe in absolute statement, knowledge of the blood response to the approaching blood. Brodsky rejected this, blocking the turn of their blood to identical revolt. The need to narrow all isolate assertion to her identity drew cords of laughter thin in Kerith's neck.

"You who are not with me oppose me," she said aloud.

The white timber tide subsided with the recoil of the moon, and Kerith walked softly into the hall. Nora slept alert behind her door.

"Yes, come in."

Kerith opened the door against the voice. Nora's wide bed.

"What time is it, Kas?"

Kerith felt the long soft caress through her body.

"About three."

She sat erect over her knees, her voice whispering against the clogged sleep of H. D. beyond in the library.

"Don't you feel, don't you believe it is possible to know an absolute, a whole realization of freedom? Freedom in every part of us. A departure from this base, from these foundations, with a perfect inner resolve . . ."

She spoke without confusion as though her voice too were masked and unknown in the veiled darkness. Nora's face was a luminous oval on the pillow.

"Yes," she whispered. "I do, I do know what you mean."

Kerith's face leaned over her knees, seeing the box factory wall sagging upon the yard.

"They are exhausted, those walls. They are done, aren't they? They can be humble, and withdraw in humility before the new assertion of life . . . the pure, pure hard beauty of that timber . . ."

She told Nora of the negro, and as she talked she felt Nora following the true beauty and force whose life she could not bring to words.

"When he turned me in his mind he denied me, but before that there was something finally given, not conjured by thought, naturally given, beyond thought."

She thought of the living silent bond that could be known, a slow glittering coil drawing one out of destruction into revealed invulnerable life.

"Words distort it," she said, turning her voice from it. But beyond the blight of her words there was no other approach, and she returned to it, saying softly:

"It is true . . . between you and me it is true . . . with the negro . . . with Soupault . . ."

"Soupault?" said Nora through the darkness.

"Yes, I believe in him, too," said Kerith, in soft amazement, "in Soupault."

They talked between slow pauses, as though each waited until the voice of the other had widened its last circle in the depths of consciousness.

"I may stay, mayn't I?" said Kerith at the end.

They turned unwearily to sleep.

"If I sleep with my mouth open you'll wake me, Kerith?"

In the morning Brodsky omitted his classes and came with Kerith to court. There was a case in broken progression at the bar. Words fluttered in the white startled mouth of a young Italian.

"My home, my business, one." The palms of his hands met softly. "One. Like this. They are one."

The full lids of the Italian were up-turned cups pouring the dark wine of his eyes upon them.

". . . when I comes in he and the wife and kid was sitting at the table. He gets up and takes the bottle off the shelf and offers me a drink, see? . . ."

The officer lounged forward on the rail, jeering.

"What's the matter, mate? What do you squeal for? Bum stuff, it must have been."

The paunch of the state swung down.

"The law says that intoxicating liquor shall not be served in a place of business."

The palms of the Italian lay gently together, eyes on the plainclothes man.

"My home . . . my business . . . one."

It was a reality from which no intangible coil could deliver him. The dark wine spilled from his lids, his palms lay gently together, his mind was isolate from the men, and his body was caught in destruction between them.

"The State versus Kerith Day."

Kerith went alone, thin and erect, to the high desk and the bar. She felt no following of eyes upon her. The unprogressive emotion of the room swirled to separate centers.

"What's the complaint?"

Kerith swayed silent.

"What are you here for?"

The paunch of the judge squatted hostile. Kerith stood away from the voice, listening to its thin uncertain sound.

"I don't know."

The judge shrugged to his papers.

"Driving with glaring headlights in traffic." He turned down to her. "Why didn't you have your dimmers on?"

"It wouldn't make any difference," said Kerith.

The judge could hear nothing.

"Says she did," said the officer lounging on the rail.

"You didn't," said the judge. "You were driving in traffic with glaring headlights."

"My car hasn't glaring headlights," said Kerith, "dimmers on or off, the lights are too weak to glare."

The officer lounged to her elbow, touching her gently.

"You pay your fine here."

Brodsky came through to her elbow and they stalked out indignant, under the fresh noon sky. He lifted his head to the bright clear blue.

"Oh, fragile lovely shell," he said, "oh, blue enduring egg in which our embryos are trapped, absorbing each other's growths, sucking each other's blood . . ."

They drove to Rebekah's house that dropped white walls like sharp dunes over the valley. Nora in blue, dark hair glowing under her hat, was settled on the grass, smoking but unreposed as though she were in a false position at rest and might leap in a moment to motion. Rebekah and her child were clad in light colorless slips, swaying in rhythmic movements against the hedge.

"Oh, lovely you are!" cried Brodsky. "Miriam like a little doe."

A thin furry stroke from the roots of the child's hair curved down between her full brown blades. Rebekah moved with heavy unpremeditated grace, gestures curiously unrelated as though she plucked them from the air as they passed. Miriam danced deliberately, slowly, as if subjected to a deliberate slow control.

"Doesn't Miriam find it *painful!*" cried Rebekah, laughing breathlessly and standing with them. Then she threw back her head, crying across the lawn: "Oh, Miriam child, shake yourself! Respond, respond to the spirit of the thing!"

A small smile triangled the child's mouth and she was propelled across the grass, away from them in grave untouched control.

"But she must have her own language," said Nora. The effort of bringing herself to her feet to stand with them had flushed her neck and her long cheeks.

"But I won't have my child saying things I don't understand," cried Rebekah laughing and taking Nora's hand to draw her to the house.

"Oh, but that's it! That's the whole secret of it! That's the whole thing!"

Nora walked with her, flushed. The heated flesh of the other woman swayed in strong full odor. And Nora walked on as though completely taken into the life of Rebekah, will-less under the assertion of Rebekah. Kerith followed with Brodsky, in impatience, in depression. She wanted to be away from the odors, the words of people.

6 Soupault had dropped away from her life with a finality that was absolute for her. It was like a conclusion of instinctive knowing, and she lived for days under a bitter deepening cloud of depression. She felt that now it was useless to care beyond Nora, to expect any further sign from humanity. And with this Nora's presence became unbearable to her, the nervous tension of Nora's hands over the meals, the wet hairs clinging in her neck. She saw Nora protruded into the future, undiminished, creating emotional apices, narrow hands insistent upon the mystic source of life.

Heat in the office pressed up as though to break her apart. At noon she lay on the bed while Nora read to her. The hill behind the box factory reared its sick hairy body upward as if in recoil from the streets. Nora's unbroken voice turned the pages of Conrad, the pure fresh words of Conrad, pure, pure through the room. Nora's fingernails were soiled on the edge of the book. Kerith lay taut on the bed with a fire of revulsion in her. She was thwarted, the pure cool voice of Nora obstructing her.

She went blindly into the office, knowing that she had come to an end. The office drew away, ended. Her defenses were consumed. But she could conceive of nothing beyond, nothing to spread new roots of strength in her.

In the late afternoon Soupault's voice from the switchboard stumbled to her meaningless. The time had passed for any sign he might have made to her. He was unreal to her now. In the evening he came, lean ankles and wrists from his clothes.

"You would have liked me to wear my uniform."

He was unreal to Kerith.

"I don't know. Perhaps you are better like this. You are not dated so. Now you have no antecedents."

They walked into the low open streets of town against the river. The bank cobbled up to the wharf street and small hotels and shops of seamen's gear. Brisk men walked the pavement, back and forth across their shop-fronts, bowing to the passers. Soupault, mistaking one, lifted his hat, leaning his face forward to respond.

"A bright beautiful evening," the man smiled, "and our suits all marked down for the end of the season sale . . ."

Soupault stepped away, smiling vaguely, closing his shoulders, his arms closing against him. He walked with an animal-like indolence, stepping quickly, his face and body masked in stolidity that set him curiously away in an insentient isolation. Sounds that startled Kerith withdrew from him. He was like a deaf man in his untouched progression. His body was frail, moving beside her, his hand to his hat with a frail uncertain droop, and his face starting forward to the salesman as if he had been sharply awakened by an abrupt gesture from life. He was like a remote animal, Kerith thought. Not a wood-animal, a quivering sensitive being, but a creature that was beyond human response, definitely beyond any suffering of the spirit.

It was what she had needed, to find him so, indifferent and absorbed in the perfect unknown knowledge of his body. It was almost a joy to feel that as far as they all were concerned, he was dead. Whatever they could know or touch of him was dead and muted, but there was a part that had been reborn to a new being, to a vigorous unconscious knowledge that was absorbed in itself. It was so with trees, the dead withered bark of trees that was mute to everyone, and then stemming within, the clear flow of white vitality from the roots of life.

At the ferry quay the *Island Queen* slothed in the river, nosing to Coney Island, gloomily cropping water. A few people had gathered at the closed plank, waiting.

"Would it be fun to go up the river?"

Soupault turned to her voice.

"If you wish."

He was outside the question, waiting for her voice to direct them.

"Yes, let us go."

The smell of blistered paint crackled from the decks and the high gnawing cry of the calliope ground above them. Couples came down the cobbled bank, girls on their stilted heels laughing. The long slope from the street to the quay became a solid bright swarm of faces, and the city roofs huddled in smoke behind.

The rope lifted and the crowd awoke to laughter, shouting close upon each other, pressing down with their bodies and cries. Kerith was caught from Soupault and swung from the narrow flow at the gangplank, under into the lowest cobbles and the low lip of river water. She was borne down on her knees, and as she fell, one heel ripped from her shoe. She sat half in water, seeing her broken boot and the streaked mud on her dress. She sat in amazement. And then with a cry of elation abandoned herself to the things, to the foul river water, and to convulsions of laughter.

Soupault's face bobbled flame-red over the blind shoulders, forcing himself down to her stricken abandon. She lifted her face to him, flushed with laughter. He drew her up by the armpits and turned, flinging their tickets in bits over the forward laughing shoulders. He brought her along the edge of people to the street. He was silent, in anger.

"You didn't mind going over," he said finally in the streetcar.

"At first, yes. I was outraged. And then it seemed the natural thing. I saw that it was the only thing that could have happened."

"Was it?" he said impatiently.

"I was better in the water," said Kerith. "Happier. If it hadn't been for cigaret stubs and sewerage it would have been good clean water."

Soupault laughed but he was impatient with Kerith's response.

"It's what happened in the war," said Kerith. She saw her long flushed profile in the car pane. "The ones who couldn't accept the whole-hearted rush, who simply didn't want it that way, were just squeezed out in the ditch."

At the shop Kerith changed to an old smock, and they went out hatless in the night. They walked swiftly up the long road to Eden Park, the dark odor of earth and leaves upon them. The sky arched over a thin deeper arch of trees, and they came to the end of trees and followed the last path that coiled in stiff shrubs above the river.

They sat, knees up-drawn, quenched in the silence. The land mellowed down from them in sensitive penetrable obscurity, and on the Kentucky bank darkness thinned, and swayed, deepening to the accentual bodies of forests. The river between clenched indurate. Hard white paths bound darkness to the hill.

And now Soupault seemed alive, his ears keen to the silence, his eyes knowing the depths of the silence between them. She felt him tightening to sound, quickening in the imperfect darkness.

"But there were others," said Soupault. "Besides that there were others—in the war."

The taste of the wind was full-fleshed and firm.

"Yes," said Kerith, "I am sure of that."

"But you don't know," he said, tightening in the silence. "There were others who marched directly up the flow. They marched against the current, against all the push of the people."

Kerith quivered to the deep stir of his voice. She felt herself at the brink of enduring knowledge. She was bewildered, slinging in desperation to the reeling silence between them.

"How? In what way?" she said feebly, her fingers quivering in the grass.

His voice rose beyond her, progressing with his own life and setting her away from him. There was a low throbbing strength in his words.

"There were a few Frenchmen who turned from Germany. I know this. They turned from Germany and marched back on Paris. They were shot down, yes, but they did that. Most of them were killed, but they did that. They turned and marched on Paris."

Kerith felt a cool wave of strength through her body.

"I didn't know. I didn't know any of them were ready for that."

She knew that to go on with Soupault it must be so, each rising separately in separate purpose. She was trembling with the silent flow of their strength.

"When we can all come to that, things will happen," she said. "Not before."

But Soupault was absent from her again. He lay away from her, uncommitted. His mind was thinking coolly, quietly over parts of his life. He remembered the cadavers in the broken butcher-shop, Frenchmen hooked up by their jaws in moonlight. They would always be clear in him, green-fleshed men dangling in their foul odor, faces leering at the moon.

"But I want just to be again of the earth," said Kerith. "Disembodied. That is all I want. Rich dark soil for the roots of new growths."

Soupault's fingers stirred soft voices in the fallen pines. Kerith felt the slow prescient movement of his fingers. The wave of her being was poised for the clear break into final knowing.

"But what will you really do?" said Soupault softly. "What will you be able to do?"

"Ah, that's it."

His fingers moved to her, touched. Silence and the long opaque coil of the river tightening down.

"I want to go away," said Kerith clearly.

"I, too," he said. "I want to go away."

Kerith's fingers lifted on his throat, shriveled in the deep glowing flame of his throat. She felt her body lifted frail and clamorous from its roots of silence . . .

Time pounded in them, rested. Her mind cooled, rested. Soupault lay apart cool, throat stemming from his dark body, touching her with his eyes.

"That is best," he said, lying cool and gentle. "That is best."

Time was a cool wind on them, smoothing the *Island Queen* from the low river curve, arc of yellow coruscate light returning, bowing under them in sedate magnificence.

7 And now she was released to action. The day passed in elation for her. Her mind was static in the conviction of action, neither turning back to the night with Soupault, nor ahead to any future for them. Whatever there was beyond this was non-existent. The past had dropped definitely away, and she was culminated in action. There was no doubt in her being as to what she would do, but her mind had not yet come to absolute resolve.

She came to the office in the evening and sat typing her own work:

> I would like to run along the street quite naked . . .
> Being naked is a fact and splendid . . .

At the outer desk H. D. typed with two fingers. Down-clanging streetcars descended past the window.

Two red lights of the night connection glowed on the switchboard. Kerith sat blouseless in the heat, her arms pointing bare and thin. They talked at intervals, back and forth, breaking into each other's work. Kerith spoke of the girl who worked in the office with her.

"Don't you think it might be arranged that Nell and I each have an afternoon off a week instead of alternating Saturdays."

He drew closed, narrowed kind and wary.

"I don't *know.*"

His machine tack-tacked on, and Kerith worked for a moment.

> I stand alone in the sun and I cry to you:
> "Come, come, for God's sake come and be awake . . ."

H. D. worked closed and contracted with fear. If he slackened his nervous taut hold on them all there would be a let-down in working progress. And working progress pounded hard into the future, pounded into success. First it had been the blueing business, and then he had been a partner in the brass business, and now it was auto repairing. No one knew how he became involved in these things. It was not by choice. He was drawn into alien activities by men more subtle than he, and when the ideal had failed, the gutted carcass was shifted to him. He worked, calling attention to the enormous death with his chaste-worded ads. Four hundred and thirty eight times he had typed: "It occurs to me that the battery in your electric car may not be standing up as well as it might to the exigencies and frequent demands that you are making upon it these summer days."

Kerith stopped her work, looking over to him.

"It's rather important," she said.

He typed blindly on.

"You see the shops are closed Saturday afternoons and Nell can't get a thing when she needs it. Now if it's my week to have Saturday afternoon free, let Nell choose whatever afternoon she wants while I work alone. And the next week I choose an afternoon, and so forth."

He typed on in his blind sightless groping, seeking an escape without really wanting to thwart them. Kerith walked to him, closing her arms tightly about his shoulders.

"*Don't* you think it would be nice?" she murmured.

His moist face pressed back on her bare shoulder, the dry roots of his scalp against her chin. His body was stifling, moist and odorous, in an old winter suit.

"But how would Nell feel about it, honey? You'll have to ask her too before I can say anything."

Kerith bent slowly over to kiss his mouth. It was as though everything in him had submitted to her. He leaned back against her, yielding his whole being to her, and she felt that his eyes were ready to flow with tears.

"But we both decided today, Nell and I," she murmured. "We decided we'd rather."

"Oh, *fraud.* No, go 'way, you're a fraud."

He leaned in her arms, laughing. The old man shuffled in from the passage, in slippers and pajama breeches. The heavy dull flesh of his torso swayed bare. He spoke pleasantly to Kerith, avoiding them with his eyes.

"Don't you think you should have something about you?"

The upright entity thrust between her and the yielding being of her father. She drew away, and the tapping of H. D.'s machine began again under his two fingers. The old man moved busily and pleasantly across the office to the open window.

"I think the shade might at least be drawn."

Kerith gathered her work slowly together.

"I can't stay here if there's no air."

She went from them into the lighted library. Nora was not alone. She sat with a cigaret and the little dogs, and Rebekah who had run in for a moment. Rebekah was slimmer, more smooth, in black, excited after her day out of town.

"The directors were having a social day," she laughed, "for the wives of the representatives. Max thought it would be good policy if I went up."

"You and policy!" laughed Nora.

"But it was amazing," cried Rebekah. "I didn't know such things could be. The factory like a palace. Everyone glowing with content. Girls and boys with swimming pools and recreation places open to them. Restrooms, playgrounds. Mothers put their youngest offspring in the nurseries, in the hands of trained attendants, while they go on into the shop to their work. Everything worked out to the last detail . . ."

"Sort of Communism, isn't it?" said Nora.

"Yes!" cried Rebekah, laughing. "Just that. Wouldn't they love it if they knew! Except grandiose," she said. "Ionic pilasters and marble drinking fountains. *I* felt positively shoddy."

"And the building up of that meant wreckage on every side," said Nora.

"That isn't important," said Rebekah. "I don't care how many go down if the cause is great enough. They broke one after the other in getting the monopoly."

"I'm afraid I'm not Malthusian," said Nora. "My curiosity, *not* my humanity, prefers that the entire population live on, even though the whole of it be insufficiently fed."

Rebekah stood up laughing.

"I'm going before you ruin my day, Nora!"

She turned back at the door to them.

"But you can't possibly object to the messenger boys flying down the long marble halls on roller skates! It simply delighted me."

Nora walked with her. Rebekah was the essential assertion, stemming up dark and glowing in her black suit. Nora felt shrunken below her in a light old dress, felt the bones striking hard and separate across her chest.

"Ah, yes, I can!" she cried, half serious. "Youth shouldn't be confined to the limits of mechanical progress!"

A flash of impatience went over Rebekah's face.

"'Confined,'" she said looking away. Then she turned to Nora, taking her hand. "We'll talk about it again. I'm beginning to have a strange faith in the possibilities of this age."

"Good," said Nora, and the short other flash of impatience crossed Rebekah's face. She hesitated a moment and then left them, smiling back.

Kerith followed Nora into the little bedroom.

"Shall we go out?" she said.

"I should love it," said Nora. They belonged to each other again. The soiled collar in Nora's neck was a bond of comprehension between them.

They came through the office and H. D. looked up from his typing, uneasy with the memory of Kerith's abrupt turning from him.

"Going out?"

"Yes, don't bother about coming for the gate."

"Why not, honey?"

He followed, putting an uneasy playful arm about Kerith. "Did you know we were going to have one afternoon off a week, muddie?" he said playfully.

"No! Really?" Nora turned dazzled to him. "Oh, I'm so glad."

She stood smiling to him, as though speechless in her gratitude.

Kerith backed the car out from mail trucks and waiting wheel-less cars. H. D. ran ahead, opened the gate, and stood small, waving after them. They fled up the hill, waited with the traffic at precise peopled crossings, and turned finally into a road darkness that expanded into gloom. The road tapered above a valley in which lights lay, disintegrate, gold shattered bits of a destroyed whole. High on the road, darkened cars sprawled in obscurity. The lamps of the Ford flashed over them, startling blinking couples apart.

They stopped above a slope that frayed into full soft trees against the sky. They walked down under the stars. Nora uttered low shivering cries of exquisite wonder, and Kerith touched the grass with her fingers and lay on the ground in the profound warmth of grass. Wonderingly Nora moved over the grass, finding her own stars in the pure confused sky. Kerith's voice moved deep in the grass.

"This I accept. This is mine. The dark subtle burden of earth."

Nora came back to her and sat with her, stroking her neck.

"I am going to go away," said Kerith, "away from the shop."

Nora quivered with recognition.

"Yes, you must go."

Her hand came close and warm to Kerith. She swallowed softly, and Kerith watched the short lovely line of her swallowing throat. Nora's voice quivered full in her mouth.

"I have made clearings in me . . . and the things that are freed in the clearings are the worthwhile things in me. I can back you up with these. I don't know what I've given you. I don't know."

Kerith felt the swoon of the flame-white sky. Her fingers moved on the narrow thin hand of her mother.

"You are the impetus, the life force . . ."

Nora stirred, wanting to acknowledge this within her.

"No, you have your own source," she said softly in a moment, knowing it was the final truth she wanted.

8 There were three unwieldy hulks of safe, high desks with stools, and the low desk with a typewriter, empty. Beyond this was the shallow office of R. C. Tarney, large window six stories above Vine Street.

Kerith came into him shaken. His hands pounced blonde on the chair arms, his eyes clung to the window. From his warm wet his cheeks burst softly.

"Brodsky spoke of you," he said.

In the clear light he was delicately colored, the hair on his temples growing up bright into baldness. His waistcoat cloth was dark and new over the low soft swell of his paunch. His warm mouth exploded:

"There's a lot to it."

The papers on his desk were flaked in thin sheets, dark-mottled with business headings. One end was weighted with a bit of artillery iron and on the edge lay a claw-handled cutter.

"There is not only the surface need of a stenographer."

He rubbed the small red mark on his forefinger.

"Business to my mind is simply a manner of living. To live well is to live wholeheartedly, altruistically. So to do business well. This business was conceived and lives on that principle. It lives well. Whoever comes into it comes with that understanding."

Kerith nodded as he came to her face, and he smiled quickly, drawn to her, feeling truth acknowledged in him.

"There is much more than the surface need of a stenographer," he repeated. "There is the need of understanding and sympathy. Sympathy with the aims of this organization. This business has a

meaning. Not only a personal meaning. It has a relative significance."

He talked simply, with fervor, as though conviction were reborn
in him as he spoke.

"There is not one article brought out from the workshop that I do
not understand and know in every shape and form of its development. The smallest pinclasp or the most intricate setting has been
part of my life for days and weeks. Its growth has been my growth.
This organization of service has become my life philosophy."

In his throat he cleared space.

"For years I have worked alone on this principle." His voice included her in his isolation. "I worked alone. But in more recent years
men of like faith and inspiration have become known to me. And I
have allied myself and my work with them. We are allied. We stand
united."

He spoke softly, waiting subdued and humble in the intention of
his creed.

"Does this interest you?" he asked, coming again to Kerith.

"Yes, it does," said Kerith. "It does."

"I think it does," said Tarney with a small fresh smile that was
like a dispensation to all routine existence. "I think you see," he went
on, "the angle which gives these smaller things a wider significance."

He spoke into the abstraction of the window.

"I have not been content to see my business progress singly, ig-
noring its relation to universal progression." He smiled whimsical-
ly. "I am, I fear, an idealist. That word I do not like. A believer, let us
say, in the realization of ideal service, and in self-realization through
service."

Kerith listened, knowing her own antithesis to that faith. It was
the experiment of Christianity that had failed for them. In every form
of their existence they opposed it. The ideal love-faith of Christian
origin was meaningless in the conditions it had erected. Love had
created this, this city was built on love, the system conceived in love,
and if there were nothing more chaste than love in the heart of man,
then they were doomed. And the doom was beautiful, complete and
perfect. Between love and doom, if there were any choice left to
them, doom was the perfect and single choice of man.

"I never dared hope to find a group of men whose beliefs would be identical with mine," he said, "and whose work would be builded on a deep foundation of faith. The kind of faith that reaches under the national differences of man to the love in their hearts. But I have been most fortunate," he went on in gentle triumph. "In England, in France, in Spain, in Italy, Australia, New Zealand, Hawaii, Portugal, Switzerland—" he held them on his fingers, "there are groups, believers. Men who are concerned with the foundations of a world understanding."

After the soft fall of his voice they sat silent. Then he began more briskly.

"We move in a circle, you see, but in a circle there is no marked center, so that we have chosen as our symbol a wheel. A wheel with a strong nucleus, with firm spokes, a moving widening wheel." He turned to his desk, the chair swinging his feet shortly from the floor. In his palm lay a small pin, wheel-shaped, with gold spokes from the gold and blue center. He moved it with the tip of his finger, leaning to Kerith, speaking simply. "This is our emblem. This is our wheel. This is the wheel of Rotary."

They sat in silence, looking down into his palm.

"It is made from my die," he said straightening back. "The number of spokes has recently been changed. This is the perfect design of it, proportion, coloring. Other manufacturers produce a similar object, but noticeably inferior. You will remark all this in time."

He settled gradually back in his breath, looking up to her, eyes curiously bright in his fragrant flesh, eyes tentacular and without subterfuge.

"This gives you some idea of what it means," he said smiling.

"Yes," said Kerith from the uncertainty within her.

"I think you understand what I've been trying to say," he insisted.

"Yes," said Kerith from her doubt, "I do."

"And that it interests you," he urged.

"Yes, it does interest me," said Kerith, "I didn't know it was being done. I didn't know it could be done in business."

"Here you will get the actual demonstration," said Tarney. "I think we can make out together. I feel the intelligence of your approach. Understanding is a priceless thing, priceless."

"And you think I might do?" said Kerith.

"We can try," said Tarney, smiling, rising. "Eighteen as a beginning. Monday?"

Kerith moved out from his eyes. "Monday."

"Monday at eight-thirty. Good."

H. D. sat at the switchboard nervously plugging the connections. His neck stretched thin to the receiver and his moist flesh twitched. He stood up from the sharp noise of the board, fumbling down with his hands.

"Here, Kerith, here's another call. Here, take it, girlie."

He crossed the room from her until the window made a cool peaked square about him. He stood looking out.

"Say, Keth, I had that family across the way all figured out. Two kids and the grown-up sister. And now if they don't go spring a small boy with a collie pup on me."

Kerith began requisition sheets. The other girl was off at lunch.

"Perhaps they're visiting."

"No, Maw came out and boxed his ears awhile ago. And anyway he has the same jerry-built dome as kid sister."

"Dad," said Kerith, "I've been offered a job."

His back narrowed into silence. And then he turned to her with a bright shy pride in his eyes, half-smiling.

"Offered a job! Well, what sort of job, honey?"

"A man named Tarney, a man Brodsky knows at the Chamber of Commerce, wants me as stenographer at eighteen a week."

H. D. sat on the desk edge slowly.

"Eighteen, a week, eh? Say fifty cents a day for lunch, that's three dollars, leaves you fifteen clear."

He sat, afraid to see her with his eyes.

"What do you want to do, girlie?" he said.

"Why I think I'll have to take it," said Kerith, "don't you?"

His soft profile lay down from his forehead, long soft nose, full rise of his lipless mouth, his chin fumbling into thin lifted softness. Kerith looked up to his eyes that drew down to her, shy and tender.

"Have to take it, huh? Bad as all that, huh?"

Their eyes came to a final knowing of each other.

"If that's what you want," he said, "you better go after it. You'd be self-supporting. As long as I can't pay you anything here you'd better go to it."

Kerith reached up, touching his cheek below his shy knowing eyes. The switchboard whirred open a small white mouth. Kerith responded.

"H. D.? Hold the wire."

Beyond his voice answering over the wire, she stirred to reach Nora. She ran into the passage and the dim living room, flashed into the voice of Nora and the long deep voice of Brodsky. She cried softly, exultingly to them:

"I am free! I am free!"

She plucked from the chair back a brilliant square of silk which was left single so that they could drop it where color was wanted. Moving with the silk she swung forward in ecstasy, arms rigid to the color, hands stretched thin in the flame. Her feet followed the procession of her arms and the quick soft steps of her hands. Her body from the hips was static, embracing the center of gravity, the unshaken core.

Softly shadowed to them in the half darkness she cried:

"I am free! I am free!"

Brodsky struck his hands together as she stood breathless in the gold-pointed darkness. Nora was strangely drunk with recognition, crying deeply:

"Ah, if you can keep that, Kerith! Hold on to it, strongly, strongly. That's all that matters."

With a full involuntary tremor, Kerith perceived that Soupault was standing apart in shadow. He came forward to light her cigaret, holding the match in his curved trembling fingers. Kerith's eyes felt down his lean wrist, down the dark flesh of his arm revealed in the sleeve. His body was so intimate to her, and yet strangely unknown. She knew that she had never known his flesh. It gave her a cold curious ease to be certain that she had never been alone with him in darkness. And then his lean hard wrist, the lean curve of flesh into his sleeve, struck throbbing notes of knowledge in her.

She looked up at him harshly.

"Did I frighten you?" she said. She was in a brilliant flaming swoon.

"No," he said. He laughed, "I'll dance too when I leave the university."

Brodsky turned to them, smiling and antagonistic.

"But don't you feel, don't you feel the university offers you a freedom—a freedom through your mind? Do you really believe there will be something better than that?"

Soupault stood smiling in bewilderment, his head sunk smiling between his hunched shoulders, and his fingers clinging to his hips. Kerith blew sharp smoke.

"If you live in your body, Brodsky," she said, "you want freedom you can feel in your body. The kind of freedom you keep so carefully in your mind seems simply done to me, worn-out. We need another kind now."

Brodsky turned away, seemingly saddened that she could dispose so wholly, so arrogantly, without knowledge.

"But things aren't absolute," he explained gently. "Don't you see? The contemptible freedom I cherish doesn't stop in the mind, not necessarily. But if it wants to begin there I can't force it down into my flesh. It just must go where it wills."

Kerith was impatient with the false truth he created for her. He accepted her always so perfectly, without perceptions for the significant clear belief beneath the confusion of words.

"Things aren't absolute," she said. "Of course. It is what I feel most strongly."

They could get no farther. She turned to Soupault, knowing so well the differences that set the two men apart. Brodsky said nothing more to the Frenchman, as though he were below notice.

"But things can begin in the blood, and come slowly to the knowledge of the mind. That is what I mean," she said presently, after the conversation had turned completely away.

"Well, *what?*" said Brodsky smiling. "Exactly what? I'm really interested."

"Why, I can't tell you," said Kerith slowly. She smiled. "Let's let it go."

9 The following day was Sunday and Soupault came again in the heat, his skin cool and immune like the gold belly of a snake. Nora talked to them of the reparations, drawing them into her bedroom where a map of Europe covered one wall and North America flapped on the door panel. She knelt on the bed pointing out the divisions of the League of Nations, dropping her slippers and stepping into the bulge of pillows to reach Poland.*

Nora's lambent presence controlled them in perfect balance. When she left them in the library, going off to boil eggs for their cold supper, Kerith was lost, feeling the central base of equilibrium withdrawn, quivering against the approach of his body.

But he stood away from her, saying slowly:

"There were no mauvais effets of your getting wet, were there? You didn't catch cold?"

"Oh, not in the least," said Kerith laughing. "Oh, no, you see I'm quite all right."

"Yes, you are, aren't you?" he said as though he were entirely absent from her.

They helped Nora pack the supper and Soupault carried the basket out through the office, down the shop stairs to the Ford. The old man emerged from his closed room to eye Soupault and to bow effulgently, "How do you do, sir?"

Kerith drove the car out, with Soupault beside her and Nora with the little dogs behind. Roads leading out made a furtive escape from the city, like dry white talons clutching the land. Cars, tortuously

---

* Established in 1919 at the Paris Peace Conference to promote international cooperation, the League of Nations was hampered in its effectiveness by the nonparticipation of the United States.

ejected from dust, clotted about the Ford. Kerith drove out of the hills, crossing the last bridge under which the river lay stagnant in the train yards, water pressed narrow between long cool streams of flowing rail.

They came into a road that turned like a ditch below trees. Kerith drove slowly, taut to the expectation of another car rocking out from the bend and pressing them aside as it lolled past. But they went on alone, in a silence that rose cool and insistent in their ears.

The land beside them was undulant pasture, purely and sensitively green. Kerith felt it flowing so, pure and sensitive, into her soul. It was a supreme requital for the fact of being, cooling the depths of her soul with pure sensitive color. She knew that in the highest moments she could come beyond humanity into a restoring soul-committance with non-human beauty. But it was so rarely achieved, rarely in the supreme fusion of sensation. And now she was open to it, accepting the long cool flow of pasture.

They left the Ford in the road ditch and Soupault carried the basket through the fence to the cropped pasture. The little dogs stopped appalled before islands of dung. The land curved firmly down to a creek. Heat was stretched between bare tree trunks, thrust apart on the sharp twigs of furze.

Nora lit a cigaret and moved from them to the creek, calling to the dogs. Kerith and Soupault followed and stood with her above the deep path of water. Under the bank a thin spawn of sand coiled yellow, widely potted by the triangular feet of duck. The creek bottom was accentuated through water, smooth with stones of a dark and strange purity. And then, around the water bend, a group of ducks came down upon them like a white burst of light. Water wrinkled back from the firm bulge of their breasts, and the little dogs lifted dazzled wondering faces to Nora for knowledge. Then in a copper flurry they whirled down upon the sand where the ducks puttered softly.

"Girls! Girls!" cried Nora, and Soupault leapt down to them. The ducks bulged away through the dark water, and Soupault came up with the dogs curled like coppery cuffs over his wrists.

They had finished their supper, their cold eggs and bread, before the first whip-poor-will cry turned like a cold observant eye upon them. Soupault could not believe in the bird and watched the obscurity for some movement of life.

"It is someone there, whistling."

He and Kerith crept out together through the wet grass. At the creek bank they stood waiting, and unbelievably near, the clear unknowing solitary cry touched them.

And now they were calm together, unwanting. They stood in the darkness almost touching, without desire. They were soundless, perfected in darkness, with the cold cry of the bird striking through their consciousness. They were in a completion of silence, indifferent and whole in their own beings. There could be no further summons from the body of one to the other. There could only be now the separate response to the thing that existed between them.

Kerith felt that they could go on inviolable in life, could they remain so, in the actual experience of the impulse of being. But it must never become a reiteration, a restatement of emotion that could only diminish to the intensity of a belief. Belief, creed. The sound of it sickened her. She would be her own being, in a full perfected knowledge of living.

"Well, why does he take life so seriously?" said Soupault.

Kerith laughed and wondered about his words. It amazed her when Soupault said sudden canny things. He seemed to emerge from his psyche of strictly non-human being.

They came back to the point of Nora's cigaret under the trees. Katydids rasped in the branches above them and these too were unknown to Soupault.

"This is your American scene, then," said Nora. He lay in contentment, close to them. His voice pressed up upon the frail inertia of leaves.

"Magnificat-ah-ah-ah-ah," holding a firm base under muted leaves.

As they sat talking at intervals, relaxed on the grass, voices rumbled upon them, and a sullen malignant mass moved down the attenuated darkness. Soupault sat up abruptly, flashing his pocket light up the pasture.

"Put out that light or we'll shoot."

They stood up in silence, shaken. The mob swung slowly down, lighting a lantern now, and muttering. Figures swung slowly down around the moving light, and the little dogs stretched back in sharp-mouthed terror.

"Got dogs too," the voice came forward.

The men were close upon them now, standing with guns and sticks in the round light of the lantern. Nora's voice trembled as she went up to them with the dogs in her arms.

"But you've made a mistake, surely, you've made a mistake."

A voice jeered from the dark group.

"Oh, no, we haven't made a mistake! We haven't made no mistake. Just get out of here."

Nora swayed in the light.

"But I don't understand. I don't understand."

The men bulged around the light.

"Well, you don't have to understand. Just get out."

Kerith and Soupault leaned, picking up the basket and coats, throwing things together.

"Oh, don't bother with them, mother. We'll go, we'll go."

"But we haven't done anything wrong here," persisted Nora, swaying with the dogs in her arms.

"It's private property, that's what it is," said the man. "And you're trespassing. That's what."

"Oh, we're so sorry," said Nora. "We didn't know. It just seemed a cow pasture."

The jeering voice came from the group.

"Well, cow pastures don't roam around loose, you know."

The men relaxed on their guns, snickering with him.

"But we only had our dinner here," said Nora. "My daughter and this young man and I. Do you mind people coming out here where it's cool and just eating quietly?"

The man shifted his gun.

"Oh, it isn't that, ma'am. But you see other kinds of people comes here. You can't tell what goes on down here. We got to be careful."

"But you frightened us badly," said Nora. "Had you any intention of shooting?"

This hardened and exulted them. They straightened.

"Sure we'd shoot, sure we would. This is outside the city limits where there's no police protection. So the law's in the hands of the farmers. We keep order out here and we got a right to shoot. You got no right to stop in any field or clearing or woods or no place."

Kerith and Soupault started off to the Ford, and Nora came up with the men protesting. Kerith started the engine, and when Nora had settled in the car, the farmers talking deferentially, almost apologetically now, at the window, she jerked roaringly out of their voices.

"More for the American scene, Soupault."

She drove hard down the darkness.

"The modern milieu, the morality of industry."

"Oh, I'll go as quick as I can," said Soupault, "I'll get away as quick as I can."

"Yes, we'll all do that," cried Kerith, "and then where will we go?"

"It's not where you go, Kerith," said Nora. "It's what you take with you."

"But I'm sick of creating worlds," cried Kerith, impatient and bitter now. "I won't sit back selecting the good parts and turning sick at the bad." Her face turned sharp. "I don't want this to go on. I don't want this ineffectual protest. I don't want people working against the established powers. They're too perfectly established. I simply want people to go off and accept a new way of life."

"Yes," said Nora, "but where can people go? Individuals have always felt that, as you do, but where can you turn but inward. Where else can you go?"

"Away from the factories," said Kerith, "away from the shops and offices. As it comes to them, to drop the tools and slowly evolve a new way of life. Establish a new superiority."

It seemed so easy to her as she said it, so almost perfected and done.

"Blow it up," said Soupault thrusting his thumbs upward. "Every city and nation and race."

Nora laughed.

"You're a good one, Kerith, to be entering a new phase of the capitalistic system in the morning."

"Well, perhaps Tarney is an individual," said Kerith, doubtfully.

Soupault carried the coats to the living room and drew away to the door. Closed silence in the little office crouched upon them. H. D. had been closed all day in the heat with the old man. Kerith was prepossessed by the dooming silence behind the door. She knew that H. D. was being consumed in the old man's intention. He would come out to them a protrusion of the old man's will.

Kerith leaned on the steps, smoking.

"Perhaps it will not always be that way," said Soupault. "Perhaps we can find a place away from the city where we can all go again."

Kerith was quiet, her mind on the men, smoking in the heat.

"Perhaps there are places more distant from the city, where we could eat again."

Kerith stood high on the steps looking down to him.

"I don't believe there is any place," she said, "do you?"

Tentative light came shallow from the opening door of the little office. H. D.'s head rounded, caught in their eyes, he smiled into "good evening," and was quenched in the shutting gloom of the door.

Soupault smiled.

"I'll go then."

He stood below in shadow. His shadow pursued him up the street, contracted and jerked nervously ahead at the street-light. H. D. peered tentatively again from the office.

"Frenchie gone, eh?"

He came out to her, closing the front door, patting her gently on the shoulder.

"Have a good time?"

His face gleamed moist above his hot clothes, and his palm dried on her shoulder, moving parched on the light stuff of her dress.

"I've been thinking over that Tarney proposition."

Fear placated the corners of his mouth. His hand rubbed dry at her shoulder.

"I've talked it over with Dad today." The turgid swing of his voice disposed of the old man's opinion. "Now in going over the items of expense, you and I didn't think of car fare, honey. Now that would eat a pretty big hole in that fifteen."

His breath came long and moist and his fingers patted into her.

"I've come to think it would be better if you stuck to the guns with me."

"Oh, no," said Kerith, stirring from him.

"Yes, honey. Better for you too. Remember that working for other folks won't be like working for your old dad." He hugged her shoulder close to him. "You work here and when you're tired you knock off and go stretch out on the bed. Don't have any car trips—

they're tiring as the very deuce, you know. And above all you've got muddie here. You can help her a lot by sticking around and cheering her up."

Kerith's mind flamed wide. The streetcar rails threshed upward and the color of light gagged in its own shrill whisper.

"Now in a couple of months things will be different here. The brake liners will be going through big and then we can all let up a bit. You stick it out here and we can make it a go that much quicker."

She felt words blocking off in her mouth.

"No, I have to take it. I have to go."

H. D. dropped his arm, narrowing.

"I need you here," he said clearly.

"But I need to go," said Kerith, "for myself, I need to go."

In the white turn of light his mouth trembled, grew back tight.

"What if *I* talked that way? Where would we all be now? Where would your mother be if I had talked like that?"

"I don't know . . . I don't know. That doesn't matter now." She clung to the door. They had never before faced each other so. "You've chosen. You've let yourself in for it. I don't think we could be much worse off. It's not mine. I've got to go on with myself."

H. D. sprang away, crying sharply through his teeth.

"Yourself! Oh, yourself! All right go on with 'yourself' then! Go on. I'm through with you."

He trembled up the timber steps and shut the door with him quickly. Kerith leaned against the open street door and grief quivered in her arms, fell released in her palms. Her mouth against the door frame fell open with weeping. She felt that all her life she had been saving him from this, and that with her betrayal of him his last defense was down. She had loved him, and she had protected him from this final knowledge that even she could oppose him. And under her grief was a cold core of wonder, amazed at his flame. She had never known this in him. And now it had taken form as his one reality. He had always interposed between them and this, an opaque shadow of being.

She thrust against the wood, her teeth in the wood until her jaw tightened acrid and still.

10 In the morning Kerith went to work for Tarney. His mouth formed slowly on his words, eyes brooding off as though committed to a visual acceptance of them.

"I want you too . . . my friend . . ." he said upon Kerith's notebook, "to become a part of that real and beautiful thing whose foundations . . . the foundations of which . . . we laid last year . . . in Colorado . . ."

Colorado boomed in his throat.

"There in . . . in that remote . . . uncivilized . . . and altruistic spot . . . no recognized authority . . . no abiding law . . . and but one immutable principle . . . that he who comes to cast his lot with us . . . shall come prepared to live beyond false prejudices . . . in perfect freedom . . . and unquestioned liberty."

Kerith looked up from her pencil, words rising eagerly in her. Tarney smiled, settled back in his stomach, softening his cigar. The whine of a fire engine throttled in the street.

"We have five hundred acres of virgin forest land," he said, speaking gently to her. "In the heart of Colorado. We have put up log cabins and when we can get away we go there. Some fellows stay all year 'round. Dropped their business altogether. There's limitless game, two lakes full of fish, and a herd of cattle—small western stock. We do everything ourselves, but there're a few landmen who work around, taking as much produce as they need in payment." He laughed behind his warm cough. "There isn't such a thing as money. Why, living there you stop thinking in terms of money."

Kerith sat nodding. It was what could be done.

"We started this three years ago," he went on, smoking gently, "and it's gone with a will. It was bound to. It appeals to the best part of man, and we're quick to stand up for what's best in us."

Are we, thought Kerith.

"But *you* come back to work afterwards?" she said.

Tarney smiled.

"Yes, come back recharged with life. Absolutely restored. The exhausted nerve cells recharged. I come back as though I were just beginning business."

He turned to his letters.

"That's personal," he finished, "with my kindest regards." He cleared his throat. "My dear Mr. Thurwall . . . I have had my designer do up an attractive sketch of the boxing glove charm in which you are interested . . . so that you may yourself judge of the careful and faithful study we have made of the glove . . . and of the special attention we have given its individual character . . . this has resulted in the production of an artistic and at the same time simple and realistic piece of work . . . if you are seeking an object worthy to serve as an expression of your esteem for manager . . . trainer or enthusiastic non-professional . . . I know you will agree with me that the 14 kt glove with chip diamond in fist is a fascinating proposition . . ."

Kerith typed in the day, hearing his voice in the private office rumbling with that of a customer, blustering to laughter. She thought of him as a possible part of progression, his actual life manifesting an approach to dissent, the perfect word of dissent to be uttered beyond him. But it was a far cry from the humble withdrawal Kerith wanted.

And yet wasn't he doing precisely what she wanted. She talked so long and so bitterly of turning from acquiescence, and Tarney was seeking his own truths and the fundamentals of his own way of life. But it was false to her, softened in his mouth. Nothing was sacred to him. And yet she loathed the common inheritance of sacred knowledge. It was always over the brink of sentiment, so that only the coldest minds could possess the pure unblemished essence of it.

A few days later they talked in his office. His flesh was fresh and pink under the sun.

"I think we have fallen—all fallen further than we know," he said. "We have forgotten our heritage, the image in which we were made. If we could only remember in every moment of thinking activity that we were created in the likeness of the Supreme Being. Man is supreme. Man is the supreme act of God . . . the hand and the heart and the mind of man penetrate and reveal all life . . ."

Ah, do they, thought Kerith. She remembered lying on the black tongue of grass, with the sharp teeth of stars plucking at her . . . the river passing, issuing from unrealized darkness . . . the dark depth of water, and her body a white flake of flesh on the dark indifferent tongue of the hill, indifferent. Only man taut as a bowstring, tense in the mystic indifference of eternal being.

One morning while Kerith sat at breakfast the old man came into the kitchen, stretching up to the shelf for matzos. He lingered at the window, breaking the delicate bread in small flakes before placing it between his teeth.

"Beautiful day," he murmured at the window, "beautiful, beautiful, beautiful day."

"Too nice to work," said Kerith. They were agreeable with each other, aloof. The old man balanced on his heels watching the cars clattering down, crowded with strap-hangers.

"We are apt to regard work in the light of a curse instead of a blessing," he said lightly, "but the majority of us would be at odds and ends without it."

The brittle matzos parted daintily in his mouth.

"Now, if you weren't working you'd be out in the Ford, eh?"

"Yes, out in the country," said Kerith. She began her tea.

The old man balanced on his heels, pausing.

"I should like it to be arranged so that you could be driven to work by one of the boys every day."

"Oh, really, the streetcars aren't too bad," said Kerith.

"Ah, yes," he said, "they're unpleasant for you."

He pattered from the sun-squared kitchen, through the wide dark room, his head covered with a small cap of black silk. When she had finished he came back to her, clearing his throat.

"I have just discussed the matter with your father." He tapped his nose-glasses in his palm. He was impressed by the ceremony of being the unspoken word between the two, now that their complete silence held them apart. "Your father has given me to understand that your employer drives you home, so in that way you escape the cars at night. Very well. At what time will you wish the car in the mornings?"

Their eyes met in blank non-acceptance of each, negating each other. "Why can I not feel gratitude for this?" thought Kerith. The old man turned away.

"Yes, it is arranged. All you need to do is to walk down and get into the Ford."

On the bare shop floor pools of grease were luminous with the bleak light that descended through the transparent roof. Cars stretched inert by the timber walls and men worked about them, men's remote voices threading through the great shop.

Kerith carried a roll of paper down to the battery workers. Their eyes and teeth struck clear white from the stain of their faces. They wiped their palms against their acid-gnawed coverings. Kerith stood with them, talking, opening out the paper.

"You know Debs, don't you?"*

Their eyes glinted white, their teeth smiled.

"Sure, Debs."

"He's sick in prison and his friends want to get him out. What do you say?"

"He was about the war, huh, the Germans, wasn't he?"

"Imprisoned on the charge of encouraging men to dodge the draft."

They moved in themselves, smiling.

"Sure, the war's over."

Their hands stained the paper, signing. They smiled away. The foreman, clean and white-blonde, came through the battery aisles, his skin brushing smooth in his crisp blue jacket.

"What is it, Miss Kerith?"

"It's a petition, Johnny. You know Debs is in prison."

His eyes looked away over the battery cases.

"Yes, I heard something about that, Miss Kerith."

---

* Eugene V. Debs (1855–1926), one of the founders of the Socialist Party of America and the Industrial Workers of the World, ran for president five times between 1900 and 1920. He garnered his largest popular vote in the final race while he was imprisoned for his criticism of the government during World War I. Convicted of sedition and stripped of his citizenship in 1918, he was released by presidential order in 1921.

"You know about it, then? Would you care to sign your name to this petition asking for his release?"

He looked back, smiling.

"I'd like to read up again about him, first, Miss Kerith. I'd like to know all sides of the question before I sign."

"You know his life has been a fight for the laboring people—all his life. He's given up everything for that, hasn't he—even his own liberty now."

Johnny smiled over the battery cases.

"So they say, Miss Kerith," he said softly, "so they say."

11 Kerith passed literature through the aisles of Labor Temple. The seats were filling with workers, laborers who lived in protest, in an opposition of hate, never coming to the knowledge that in them was all resource and strength. She had known their sons well, and they in their sons denied the potent beat of their blood. In place of the existent injustices they wanted a labor superiority, in the finer minds it was equability, but always the cities to remain, the factories inviolate in spirit. Nowhere was there courage to know that only in complete rejection could there be change.

But beyond this quiescent protest of labor, there was nothing. If one was opposed to this quiescent protest of labor, there was nothing to stand with. Until the establishment of a new priority, there could be no constructive art. Painting and writing and sculpture progressed to a supremacy of technique, or to a conscious identification with primal impulse, stirring a little eddy of current in the bog of civilization. As for architecture, it had ceased to be. It might have been the most exciting of the experimental approaches to life, but only architecture, in that phase of it, had had the humility to withdraw from being. Even the steam radiators that *might* have expressed so much, were now "the radiator classic." "So repeating the chaste lines of classic architecture that it may justly be regarded as *an object of art.*" And if industry, the only erect thing in civilization, wouldn't take the responsibility of its own creations they were in a bad way indeed.

If one acquiesced in the life-conditions it was possible only to side with labor. Labor was stirring for the complete break, but it would be years, it might never come to the break. And labor was set against itself. The most oppressed working man could write to the daily press:

> I was glad to see your editorial on Lenin. Only fearless exposition of the greatest maniac the world has ever known will check the rising wave of Communism in this country.

If only there were a rising tide of belief in the country, thought Kerith. Let it be Communism. Let it be anything that has strength in itself and denial of the unimpassioned acceptance of their being.

A worker passed Kerith, his arms filled with pamphlets, distributing literature. Kerith stopped him, smiling.

"Did I forget to give you an usher badge?"

He shook his head, drawing her aside to his voice.

"There's a chance of the place being raided. Steffens . . . Foster . . . dangerous speakers." He turned back the lapel of his coat. "Got my button in here out of sight."

In the back of the hall Nora was standing, her cheeks flushed with the people.

"It's filling up like wild fire."

They stood watching the doorway where people bobbled over the shoulders of the ticket taker. Soupault gave his ticket and ambled shyly to them.

"Oh, but you weren't to have come!" cried Nora. "I think this is unwise, unwise."

"We can find him a back window," said Kerith.

"Oh, but there's so much at stake for him," said Nora. "If anything happens the university will be done with him at once. He'll just have to clear out—or be railroaded out."

"So much the better." Soupault smiled. He came with Kerith to pass programs.

"Well, why *did* you come?" said Kerith, walking with him.

"It was more interesting than staying away," he said.

It was a matter of not caring to him. She thought of Brodsky sensitive to the energy of being, suffering in the perceptions of his mind, always experiencing the perfect issue of suffering; Brodsky awed by his mind and the created beauty in knowledge.

"Why, if I was simply indifferent," she said, "I don't think I would have taken the trouble to come."

He smiled.

"I didn't want either to come or not to come," he said. "It was a choice of two negations. So I came."

"Don't you think it's rather futile to feel that way about things?" said Kerith.

"I didn't think about it," he said. "It was the way I felt."

"And that's the way you feel about things in general," she said. She was impatient with his apathy. It was more than indifference. It was the ultimate drifting to the mould, the dooming apathy of life. "You just don't care one way or the other," she said. "Labor or not labor. You'd simply let things drift any way they would."

"Well, I don't feel I can do very much about it," he said.

Kerith was set away from him in a belief in action.

Beginning in the hush, Steffens stood on the platform, tip-toe, stretched to his words. His body yearned and broke in the famine, the stark pain of Russia. With his fingers taut, he talked of Lenin, the workers, acknowledging the white isolate faith in men and not the bitterness of opposed classes. Kerith felt his truth flaming in every part of her.

As he talked his voice wore thin, the threads of it slowly unraveled. He swayed to his hands. He was the word of love thrust on the lips of life. As he talked, love became a cry flung from the defeated body of Russia. Kerith held words in her throat. Defeat. Russia. Defeat. In accepting man as worker, Russia had accepted defeat. The cry stirred a strange courage in Kerith. Through the failure of the word, truth could be struck to the roots of world consciousness.

Foster spoke, blood and bone of the workers' protest. It was so simple as he gave it to them. There were the plutocrats, there were the workers. There was no more subtle division than that of man. Voices howled to the rafters with his old-regime Russian laborer who was now foreman of a gang of old-regime "plutes." They hugged themselves, howling. That was what they wanted.

Steffens sat in the Ford with Nora, and Soupault took the wheel, Kerith coming in over the piles of literature.

"Wouldn't you be very much more comfortable back here?" said Steffens. His mouth had turned winsome under his beard. He sat with his head on one side, his eyes bright and restless as a bird. "I always feel that the driver should have as little as possible to divert him."

They laughed, but he sat grave, eyes unfaded.

"Why do you leave us at once?" said Kerith. "We need you here. We need everything you have to say to us."

Steffens eyes turned gentle and winsome.

"But you see I have only one speech. And of course it wouldn't do to say the same thing over and over, would it?"

At the hotel entrance they left him. He walked with a weariness that bowed him, clear, proud freedom limited to existent life. They drove from him to the shop, but he was like a spell upon them. Nora made coffee, talking, flushed and eager.

"Superb! Superb!"

Kerith paced the room, still flaming.

"The ground is cleared," she repeated, "the ground is cleared."

Nora and Soupault sat smoking and taking their coffee.

"It seems to me very much messed up," said Soupault.

"But cleared of all illusion," said Kerith. "Lenin gives the perfect application of the system. Depressing. Horrible. Not the famine, not the killing—but the whole committing of man to labor. Nothing better than labor. Ameliorating the conditions of life under the supremacy of labor. But now we can reject it. Now there is room for a beginning."

"If the laborers could leave the factories," said Nora, "establishing their own shops. You say to ignore the present system and this they could do in setting up their own factories for the making of only necessary or beautiful things. There wouldn't have to be cheap beads and ugly clothing."

"But that isn't the best we can do," said Kerith. "It isn't the best."

In the pause of their voices they heard a car drawn up at the door. "Rebekah."

Nora went quickly from them, into the street. It was dark and she sat in the car telling Rebekah of the meeting.

Soupault stood by the lamp lighting his pipe.

"It was what they wanted," said Kerith, walking in the room. "Foster with his rest homes for the workers and his variety shows."

Soupault puffed darkly.

"Well, if you're talking of action," he said, "it's Foster rather than Steffens."

"But where is there action?" asked Kerith. "Foster talks and the men listen and go back to work and nothing is done."

"And Steffens talks and they don't understand," said Soupault. Kerith paused.

"That's where Steffens is wrong," he went on. "If he wants to reach the workers he should use the terms they know. The actual reforms of Foster are their language."

Kerith was tense.

"But the change must come in their hearts, Soupault. It's that that Steffens is saying."

Soupault shrugged.

"They're more interested in the safeguarding of their old age."

And now his apathy angered her.

"You can't give them a new vision by talking about it," said Soupault.

Kerith was in a quiver of hatred against him.

"So as far as you're concerned you'd say nothing," she said. He was standing close to her, watching her face. "You're willing that things should go on just as they are?"

"Well, I can't do very much about it, can I?" laughed Soupault.

As he spoke she lifted her hand and struck his face full with her palm, striking the pipe from his mouth. He stood still a moment, in anger, and then he laughed, stooping to lift his pipe from the floor.

"Of course that doesn't change my mind," he said, coolly.

Kerith stood apart, watching the curve of his hands solicitous over his pipe. He was so complete in life, unconfused, knowing his own center. In this he was like Nora. They were both of them completed, revolving from her on their own perfect axes. And beyond them she did not care, but they were moving from her in the impetus of their own axes.

She stood watching him, knowing this, and an overwhelming tenderness filled her. She came to him, putting her arms softly about him. He smiled down on her, remote, a cool unquestioning smile from his pointed satyr-like face. She pressed him close to her, swaying. Her mind was gone under a pure tide of darkness.

12 When Kerith came suddenly into Tarney's room, the deep bottom drawer pulled forward held bottles of bright liquor. Tarney smiled, and leaned away with the ash of his cigar. He coughed. His eyes lifted bright to the papers she had brought him.

"It's going to be possible to pipe the cabins this summer."

He drew up hard to his cigar.

"Wilderness without and private baths within. Will you get all the literature you can on plumbing fixtures?"

He leaned to snap the drawer in place, looking up to her, voice on the bottles.

"You agree with me, doubtless, that life and all it offers is open to the man who does not abuse it."

Kerith looked at the closed drawer.

"Even to the abuse of the law?" she asked, laughing.*

He smiled.

"Will you take some letters now?"

Kerith went for her notebook.

"There's something a little private this morning."

He motioned to the door, indicating the beyond stooped backs over the ledger desk. She closed the door on them. He paused.

"This on plain letter paper, Miss Day. Addressed to the City Hall, Chief of Voluntary Police."** He relaxed in his own fresh warm presence. "On Sunday afternoon . . . August thirtieth . . ." he dictated,

---

* The Eighteenth Amendment to the Constitution, mandating Prohibition, was in effect from January 29, 1920, until its repeal on December 5, 1933.
** The volunteer Home Guard was organized in 1917 as an arm of the Cincinnati city government and was made up primarily of business and professional men, who assisted as their "patriotic duty" in situations like floods and police strikes.

"while driving my car on Madison Road between two and three o'clock . . . a large old style Packard touring car with top lowered drove out Madison Road at a terrific rate of speed . . . there were eight men in the car and indications were that the driver was under the influence of drink . . . I set chase at once and although my speedometer for the space of four minutes registered a rate of fifty-five miles an hour . . . I was unable to gain upon the other machine . . . which was continually in sight careening some blocks ahead . . . I noted however the license number . . . which I hereby enclose for your future use." Tarney turned a quiet edge to his voice. "That is to be unsigned. Simply, 'Number 10.'"

His hands moved soft on his vest. He was lost in remote thought, coming back to her abruptly, making a bright movement to her to open the door. He turned to his letters. Through his first words a girl came in from the factory. The skin on her throat was gold-pored from the brushed dust of jewelry. Tarney spoke kindly.

"Good morning, Mary. What can I do for you?"

Her hands clawed on her hips, her voice thrust from her sharp.

"I'm going to lay off, Mr. Tarney."

"What's the trouble, Mary?"

Her eyes were sharp on him but dark with pain. And she was refusing the pain, refusing the submission to it, and turning her body sharp and angry upon them all.

"I'm sick, Mr. Tarney. I've worked hard and the conditions ain't perfect. It'll be hard for you because there's no girl trained to the work I do, but it may teach you something about conditions."

Tarney softened his cheeks, smiled.

"Come, come. Let's not hold malice against each other. You're not well? What's the trouble, Mary?"

Her feet were slack, submissive, under the protest of her ankle bones.

"I'm sick as I very well can be, Mr. Tarney. I've been with you a pretty good time." She looked at him. And then she said suddenly and almost without bitterness, "If I hadn't been with you so long I wouldn't be sick."

Tarney stretched his short clean legs under their sharp creases of cloth.

"You don't get enough air, Mary. I know that. Now I suppose you come to work in a crowded car and go home the same way." He swelled with her unsubmitting nod. "Now, why don't you make a point of getting up a few minutes earlier every morning and walk down to work? Saturday afternoons you can spend out in the open, walking, Mary, forcing clean air through your lungs. You'll feel made over. How about it, Mary?"

"Walking's no good for what I got, Mr. Tarney."

Tarney moved an elbow.

"Nonsense. I never heard of anything a good brisk walk wasn't good for. Now before you decide to lay off, you think over what I've said. Tonight instead of climbing into a stuffy car, you take a good brisk walk up Vine Street. I'll vouch for it, you'll eat your supper as ravenous as a wolf. You'll feel made over, Mary."

"Wouldn't take me home in your car, would you, Mr. Tarney?" she sneered at him, including Kerith in the long hostile sneer of her eyes.

"That'll do, Mary," he said gently. "You think over what I've said."

In the silent break of her going, Tarney turned to Kerith.

"There is a prevalent fear of treating one's employees as human beings, appalling fear. People do not consider them as a human problem, as individuals to be approached as individuals. It was a malicious thing to have created and to keep alive the feeling of class. We are all workers, all potential anybodies. If you think of it in that way your first instinct is to respect everyone."

At night he drove Kerith to the shop, swinging through traffic.

"Yes, we'll pipe the cabins."

Kerith watched light powdering fast through the windshield. She felt they were approaching the perfect resistance. She saw the control of his mind manifest through his body, the fair firm control of his hand on the wheel, dropping quick as steel on the glittering gears. They spoke so kindly, with such sympathy, one to the other, the genteel hand firm of their minds. And yet she knew there was the under approach to perfect opposition. It began physically in them. She felt herself dark and sullen beside his round wrist ruddy from the lip of the glove, her high nose like a great sullen beak and mark upon her.

"Queer how I dream about that place!" he said, laughing.

"Quite right," said Kerith.

He smiled, swung clear at a corner.

"You do think so, don't you, Miss Day?" He was forcing this upon her, because theoretically he admired her. She worked well and she was intelligent, and he really wanted her sanction of this. But if ever the genteel hand released him, he would know how profoundly he hated her.

At the shop he leaned back, smiling down to her as she descended.

"We are doing big things," he said gently. "Our day by day menial plodding means something else. The channeling of the unbroken currents in life. It is the beauty in materialism," he said. "I believe in it."

Soupault was waiting in the library and talking with Nora.

"I wondered if you'd come out to dinner."

Kerith pressed her lips, turning to Nora.

"I don't know."

"Do," said Nora. "It's not pleasant eating here in the heat."

Soupault moved.

"But of course you'll come too, won't you?"

Nora softened, turning graciously to him.

"You're very kind. But you see I'm not dressed. And then there's the dinner to prepare for Mr. Day and his father."

"Oh, yes," cried Kerith. "Yes, do come, mother. I'll only go if you will."

But in her heart she was willing Nora away from them.

"Yes, yes," said Soupault. "You will come."

Nora was turning to be with them, away from the men. But she shook her head.

"No, really, really. I must get dinner. And I'm rather tired, too. Some other time. Yes. But tonight I really wouldn't enjoy it."

Kerith stopped in Nora's room as she left, finding Nora propped reading on the bed. She leaned to kiss her, and Nora's eyes were wide open upon her through the kiss, staring wide and knowing into her eyes.

"You won't be late will you?"

Kerith's hand quivered on the door.

"Oh, no. Early. I'm weary."

She went out in a strange quiver of distrust to him. He had become the unfathomable danger. Nora behind her was safe and gentle, waiting in her room. But Kerith was drawn on to him, flowing into the unfathomable depths of her fear. And Nora closed in her room, knowing.

She smiled, touching the firm lip of his palm.

"Shall we be off?" she said.

His room closed about them like a fist. Words could open the fingers of the room, uncurve them separately from the palm. But Soupault did not speak, his body long and white, deepening to ochre at the armpits and breasts. She thought of words that could uncurve the future, sounding them in her throat. And then she set herself in silence in the moment with him, immutable, willing against any be-yond knowledge, accepting the solid grace of the closed moment. But her will sapped slowly away, abandoning her, and suffusing her mind with division.

"It is not enough to *be* so . . . this . . . expression from the root impulse . . . what is *this* . . ."

Her fingers turned cool and curious, seeking the unknown roots.

"I *cannot* give myself up to this . . ."

Soupault had lighted the delicate flame across the gas logs in the hearth, and they stood in the cool black air, talking and stretching their bodies.

13 Brodsky brought her a dwarf turtle under a vermillion-eyed shell. The wrinkled green arms, bright yellow-ringed from the creased wrist to the elbow above the sharp green toes that pricked in her palms. The bitter little poisoned face lifted, straining, as though he would strain himself out of his own psyche, and into a new set of conditions.

Brodsky leaned above the stricken panic of the turtle bowling over her palms. He looked down at Kerith, and then drew up, moving away from her silence. He stood across the room lighting his pipe.

"I tried to get you on the phone before and since. I had too much work on hand to break away for the Steffens meeting."

Kerith looked up, seeing the flesh curving down pale from his shallow eye-pits, the smooth thick tip of his nose.

"But really you wanted there to be that in the way, didn't you? You really wanted that, or anything in the way, didn't you?"

Brodsky sat down almost wearily, facing her, dropping one hand on the thick swell of his leg. He laughed suddenly, in slow whispered gasps.

"I'm coming to be afraid of being near you!" he said. "This precipitance—it sets me against you."

"But you are against me," said Kerith.

Brodsky lifted his hand to his face, leaning his face in the shadow of it. His flesh hung heavy and dull in the shadow.

"I wonder if you'd know what I was talking about," he said, "if I talked of the simplicity in accepting the pure joy of the state of being."

Kerith waited.

"Taking moments simply as they come—knowing the essence of life in your mind and transmitting it to action by the fact of whole being—not solving anything—"

"I don't suppose I do, actually," she said, "do you?"

He wondered.

"I want to," he said presently. After a moment of quiet, he said: "If you were sexless you simply wouldn't interest me."

"No," said Kerith, "I know. It's because I don't suffer allegorically. You want me symbolic something."

"You are," he said. "Youth-conscious."

"No," said Kerith. "Me-conscious."

"Quite as annoying," he said.

"I annoy myself more than anyone," she said, smiling falsely and prettily at him. She was being consciously so whimsical and quaint with him, and all the while impatient that he could destroy even a part of her.

He got up suddenly and walked to her, his hands swaying heavy and obscene before him.

"I am wrong too," he said. His voice, so close to silence, startled through her. "But it is not in my blood . . . there is nothing I can do. You see there is nothing I can do now."

He came to her, dropping his white broad palms on her shoulder. Kerith felt her shoulders piercing the flesh of his palms.

"I want . . ." he said. "The utmost of what you and I can be to each other. I must say this."

He leaned, forcing his words, his enormous terrific weight on the points of her shoulders. She couldn't believe in him, and she wanted to be from under him, from the probe of his voice, the full white flesh of his palms seeking down to break in her flesh and fuse them. His agitated silence braced upon her.

"But we are identified," she said. Her shoulders stirred.

"Yes, but beyond that," he said, his voice blinded with the pain of facing them. "This is the beginning. Beyond this there is something else. Marriage . . ." the word was bitter to him. ". . . marriage . . . or whatever it may come to."

"That I don't understand," said Kerith.

Brodsky's eyes leaned blindly upon her.

"I feel that to establish something, anything between us, it would have to be so. Between you and me, I feel things would have to be accepted on some permanent basis."

"I don't want anything permanent," said Kerith, "not anything."

He swayed from her, relieved into laughter. But Kerith was stirred now, reaching for words to touch him.

"If we can progress to something, I want it," she said. "If there is an inevitable progression for us."

"Well, what sort of progression?" said Brodsky. "Of course I can't know . . ."

Kerith felt the deep perilous flow in him that released could wholly submerge them, and then came the destruction of his words upon them.

He left her, walking to the closed window, palm on the pane blurring the clear substance of night. He waited for her voice, restive. Kerith walked eagerly in the room.

"We ought to have known it, if any sort of sub-human relation is possible between humans, we should have had this between us. But in one way or another we've just not moved on together. We've been in an absolute cul-de-sac, don't you feel that. As far as the other is concerned, I do feel that we've been quite ended." Kerith talked, repealing the sound of her voice. "And I do feel that we've failed outside of ourselves, even though I do believe that you've been afraid to go on with me to anything else. Do you believe that, Brodsky? Do you think we can go on now?"

And she knew that were false too because she could be talking so to him only if they were finally done with each other.

"I do want to know," she insisted.

He turned to her, and his body broke suddenly to her released. He lifted her hands, pressing them upon his warm soft throat and mouth. He bowed over her, speaking deeply, softly. But Kerith was untouched, drawing away from the warm heavy glow of his throat. She knew only the dry unkindled fear in him, and his body over her turned offensive with the obscene vermin-like fear that scurried in panic in his blood.

The change flashed in him, and he lifted his chin, his shoulders lifted and sighed down full. He moved away, talking suddenly, and his voice moved lightly across the room, excluding her. Their voices approached, clear and unviolated, and then the two walked out together, up the street-slope into the beginnings of Avondale, silent in the dark stretches between the haughty lights.

The Conservatory was mute, its concert dome rolling like a bald white eye through the trees. In Mount Auburn houses spewed light, and two water towers bulged their solid trunks against the sky. Wet wind made a gesture of silence to the abandoned world.

"But it is not late," said Kerith, wondering over the silent streets. "Just ten."

Perched on a little grass run, a brick house huddled between wider houses. On one side, a yellow clear square, like a hanging mirror.

"That is where Soupault lives," said Kerith. She stopped and looked up. "That is the light in Soupault's room."

Brodsky stood faintly smiling.

"Shall we go up?"

Kerith drew near to his arm, smiling.

"Yes, shall we?"

They walked into the dark porchway and the wind swung under the arch against the wall. Kerith touched the heavy knob and the door sighed wearily, heavily back. Light came inadequately down the shallow stair pit, and they mounted softly to the door that framed light in the transom. Beyond someone stirred on a chair. Kerith's whisper flashed up the light.

"Soupault."

Movement crossed quickly to the door. Kerith and Brodsky stood apart, amazed.

"Halloo!" Soupault stood against light. "Come in."

He was thinly, nervously elated. In his room there was the white iron bed, heaped table, and three electric globes hanging at angles like sparse fruit on the lean twisted vine.

"I have been doing my thesis," said Soupault, giving them cigarets.

Newspapers were spread open on the floor. He glanced down.

"I've wet these," he said, "and when they dry the pictures will be colored. The colors come out with the wet."

He searched outside himself for things with which to divert them, bringing them a tin box that moved with the thick sound of buttons. When he took off the lid a few rolled over in their hands, heavy artillery buttons buckled with silver, and bright jade buttons on tri-color ribbon.

There was a sharp patter of rain against the window and wall, and Soupault sprang up to lower the glass. He turned back to them, dusting his hands against each other.

"Shall we go in downtown," said Soupault, "for hot cakes and coffee?"

They went eagerly out under the dark sharp rain. Streetcars jangled dismally past with people huddled in them, their faces blurred and non-human at the window panes. In one street a main had broken and men worked under lantern light in the thick yellow clay.

"Water mains," said Kerith, "curving bodies to service . . ."

Brodsky laughed, jerking his heavy head.

"Ah, what you want . . . like the savages, dance out with wreaths in our hair, beating our hands in rhythm, singing 'the main is broken, the main is broken, we shall heal the main'—and dance all night and drink and in the first flush of dawn dance homeward singing, 'peace, peace, we have healed the main!'"

The first streets of town straggled away to dark cluttered ends, but in the brackish fling of rain there was challenge. Kerith held out her hands to it, laughing, dancing backward before the men. Soupault broke suddenly into wide delicate steps, bending his knees, dancing with his elbows up and out. Kerith stretched her arms to the dark mean houses.

"Come out," she chanted, dancing before them, "come out, sleepers, and dance with us . . . come out . . . see the walls dripping away to the gutters and the gutters running away to gold . . . our steps striking new paths while the pavements drip away to the gutters . . . come out, sleepers, breathe new odors with us . . ."

At the street corner Brodsky turned from them, smiling, giving them his hands.

"You won't mind my not eating with you?" he said. "The rain—the rheumatism, you know."

He smiled, turning from them, walking vague and ponderous into the lights and rain.

14 Kerith drove the Ford to the Railroad Workers' Outing. In the rear seat Nora talked and Soupault sat in front looking ahead to the low fields in which timber halls were caught between the opposed currents of people.

The road was sharp and steep into the fields, and cut by a train crossing. Kerith drove recklessly always, and yet with a firm agility that gave Nora, who was timid of careless speed, perfect faith only in her. But Kerith felt Nora tightening behind them as they came to the tracks, her feet gripping forward. The car was descending with such unbroken speed, as though it could never be stopped, and sensitive to her fingers, with a sardonic evil response, in perfect unity with her and in perfect opposition to any other command. They came down upon the tracks in the full swing of speed, Kerith thrilling with the approach and the firm glorious sweep of track. And then, what she had wanted, the great black beast of an engine coming down like a miracle, almost upon them. It was more like a nightmare to Nora, but Kerith was past all thought of them now, thrilling to the sardonic flash of response from the little black quivering car. They would stop just in time. She would not shatter its breath with the panic-strength of clutching the brakes and forcing the sharp electric shudder of death through it. The engine was like a great looming cloud sweeping down upon them, but Kerith would not jam them out of motion.

They came almost to the rails along which the train swung, and Kerith's hands moved quietly over the levers, her foot pressing softly down, and the Ford stood meekly there with its nose almost touching the big roaring dragon as it passed, and the flashing cars.

Kerith was quiet and thrilled with this, knowing that her body had scarcely moved to stop them, and that it was the bond and belief and pure subjection between herself and the car that had willed them into stopping. She might have sat there, she thought, and not lifted a finger, and yet the car would have stopped because it was in perfect response to her, and she was the attractile body drawing it to her direction and will.

When the train had passed them and they were again in the road, Nora was still breathless, but really unafraid. She didn't feel that anything final could ever happen as long as someone else had a firm hold on things. If Soupault had been driving, Kerith would have been mad with fear. She couldn't quite trust anybody. But Nora was never really afraid as long as the responsibility was not on herself. It didn't seem possible to her that she could actually do these things as well as other people did them.

They left the car in the field and walked in among the people, children running warm through the crowd. In the dance hall pounding feet carried dust from the churned paths until its gold choking brilliance clouded up to the windows. Girls' throats stemmed clear from the dry tight suck of their clothing. Their bare arms pressed the men's insolent bodies to their rhythm, their bare fingers pressed, sentient.

Under the trees the painted swings fell high, contracted. Girls standing in them swinging cried aloud, heads down, bare arms gripping. Men scattered beneath, shifted and smiled, seeing the girls' bodies retching at the wind.

"Hey, Mabel, keep your skirts down, keep your skirts in!"

Girls screamed, pulling fiercer at the ropes.

Above the opening coil of water girls and men sat together tossing orange peels away. Heat throbbed pauses in the girls' laughter. One youth's eyes wandered moist in his stretched white skin.

"Don't look in there, you'll see something you're not looking for, I warn you."

His eyes, moist with mirth, held ochre in the corners. The girl opening his wallet looked up, clear-eyed.

"I know. A photo of some other girl."

His eyes found the other men's eyes, satiate, obscene.

"Never mind what. Don't look in there. I've warned you."

The afternoon light turned clearly on the dark bed of water. A tree bowed over the stream, drifting long tangled moss-hair. The gnarled ends of hair turned glass-sharp under water, the earth under water lying deep and fragrant as wild violets. Leaves of mullein plant spread metal-stiff in the cold flow, blossoms hanging ripe and heavy with seed.

Soupault stood away, and they sat silent, watching the bright cruel beauty of flame curving down to water, running on the trunk in sharp copper veins, break near the other bank, and then hiss into a slow low linger of smoke.

Soupault lifted the hard threads of burned moss.

Nora stood up crying: "The tree didn't burn!"

"But only the moss burned," he said brushing away the charred clinging hair. The fresh bark lay unbroken.

They walked up the bank to the hard beat of light and music. In the field there was no night. The white odor of flesh and damp secretions under the white light. A girl's silk blouse hung slack on her shoulders and a boy from the crowd turned, slipping his hand down over her moist flesh. She ran laughing, flushed. Men pressed through the crowd, eyes twitching; women with pendulous pregnancies, hands stroking sickly flesh. On the outer side of the dance hall lewd words were chalked in white.

They came into the Ford and a committee member leaned in the window, chatting with Nora.

"Glad you came," he said, nodding to her as they started. "Glad you came. Wish we could have these outings more often. Good for us all." He smiled at Kerith. "Good for the youngsters."

15 With local elections in November there were nightly meetings at Labor Temple. Kerith waited, watched the men drifting out, men's faces pointing sharply away from their life-timidity or beaten to the break of their backs. They were coming away from discussion of conditions, the talking up of plans. And under their words were the drugged potencies of their bodies. She wanted their bodies erect in a strong tendinous march from the cities. The buildings could achieve significance then, standing stark, interpreting the new turn of a people. She thought of factory wheels choked blonde with rust, windows gone under the wind.

She leaned against the glass, crying aloud to them in the empty car.

"Why are you motionless, blood?"

She saw the veins in their throats, hard and blue with the stagnation of their blood. But beyond her voice she knew the enduring yea-thunder in them, yea to the breaking of man, yea-thunder of labor, yea above labor.

And she was motionless too, because she was only spiritually opposed to what they accepted. It was impossible that the abstract protest of the spirit could evoke any final change. The material of life must be broken up, to be recombined, with as definite a consciousness of its possibilities as any artist had of his problem. It was that awareness, not a mental or spiritual awareness, but the hard physical awareness that they all must have clear in them through the need of their lives. The life she wanted was a hard physical one, with the land, or with the sea. She liked to know her thin hard muscles were ready, crouching under the skin, and her mind wanting the complete rhythmic oblivion of wind and work. She thought she could be cold and worn with work if she were only out of the protest and the choice between the two extremes which one had to accept if one stayed. She could be happy getting old before her time and thin with work, if she were only absolutely away.

She thought of Brodsky in the isolation of his own life. She felt that now she could go to him, in recognition of him as a separate isolate being. She wanted to make immutable to him the perfect salute, the clear acknowledgment of him in the moment. And as Nora came down from Labor Temple talking, the bulk of Brodsky leaning to his cane was limping forward with her and the others. He turned when he saw Kerith in the car and moved away to his streetcar corner, but Nora cried after him.

"Oh, but you'll let us drive you home. You're not well. We can take you home."

He drew back.

"But you'll be filled up," he said.

"Oh, no, there's room, there's room." She followed the others into the Ford. "In front with Kerith, there's room, yes, there's room."

He came heavily, painfully into her. The streets, in movement, were dark, jolting him. Voices crowded in the car behind. Brodsky sunk inert in his body.

"I have been busy at work," he said to Kerith's voice.

"I have needed you," said Kerith.

Brodsky drew away impatient, sunk in his heavy flesh.

"How have you needed me?" he said. "How *could* you have needed me?"

Dark clattered up against the lights.

"There is some way in which we can come together," said Kerith.

He stirred.

"I can't, I simply can't go over it all again," he said. "I'm simply not ready."

They were silent a moment, and then he leaned forward on his arm, his face hanging between them. He spoke deeply.

"Tell me," he said.

His face hung between them like a deep tender caress upon her. Kerith spoke quietly over the wheel.

"I believe we can assert our own life, our own antithesis to what now exists. If we are ready, ready to relinquish everything. Education, art, everything to go down before the assertion of life. I want this, more than anything, I want this. I want you to believe in this with me. There are no new continents. There is only the final need of making this possible. The deepest potency of man is ignored in this civilization. There is some other way, Brodsky, there is something else."

He sighed, shifting his shoulders.

"Yes," he said bitterly, "the reduction of us all to elements. You can't do it. You know that. It's futile. It's wrong."

"No," said Kerith pressing her voice softly upon him. "If beyond our relation with each other we can be identified with this, Brodsky, we can come to a new experience of life. We can go forward separately in this to a new way of life."

He sat in silence, but without hostility now as though awaiting the final invulnerable word from her. It seemed to her so sure, so inevitable, the simplicity of the way that was on the breath of opening to them.

They had come to his rooming house and he picked his delicate and tremendous way out from them. He stood on the walk, leaning, smiling to Kerith, nodding his white heavy face to them. Kerith was fascinated by the white mask of his face and the clear dark flame in his eyes.

Kerith drove the others into Clifton, and Rebekah came with them to the shop, lingering. Her own car would stop down later.

In her room Kerith lifted her arms before the mirror, turning.

"I am thin."

Nora relaxed smoking, and Rebekah smoked from her chair. Kerith saw them reflected, turning slowly before them. She listened to Nora and Rebekah, the swing of their voices in her mind. Rebekah's voice drew away static.

"I want you to hear my first case, Nora. That you know."

Kerith felt the firm thought of Nora acknowledging Rebekah, turning to her in love.

"Oh, I want to, I want to."

Kerith brushed her hair, short strokes from her brow to the lifted ends.

"How does it feel," said Nora, half grave, "to be on the right side of society?"

"Strange for me, Nora. The Republican Luncheon yesterday when I spoke. Hostess for the directors' wives. It didn't seem me."

"No, it doesn't seem you."

Rebekah laughed.

"Ah, it's amusing too! I didn't think I could make as good speeches for a Republican Congressman as I did for the Federal Amendment."

"Yes, you meet the needs as they come up. That is rare wisdom, and rare ability. You face the needs of your life as they come up."

Rebekah was almost impatient with Nora's response.

"And what do you think *you* will do?" she said smiling. "Do you think you'll be able to go on with labor?"

Nora's lip grew slowly under her cigaret.

"I don't see how I can go on with anything but labor. Your republicans and your democrats and all the rest of your politicians seem sterile to me. There's nothing to expect from them, is there?"

Rebekah nodded.

"Well, of course, labor too, labor's being betrayed by its own leaders. At every turn the interests of labor are being sold out, you know."

Nora lay relaxed, looking out of the window from her pillow.

"That's why there's need of what we can give. As far as I can see, there must be an equal chance given the workers. If they want education, want arts instead of trades for their children, if they want to form societies . . . why are the I.W.W. members jailed and the Rotary members exalted* . . . and in the courts there must be minds, it seems to me, who are unprejudiced, unbiased. That it seems to me is the biggest need. That of courage among the clear and brilliant minds . . . minds that can't be bought. I don't think there's much hope for any of us, workers or whatever we are, until we can feel that."

Rebekah leaned forward, eager and tense to Nora. She laid one hand on the bed, pressing down until the knuckles creased white.

---

* The Industrial Workers of the World came to be known as the Wobblies. Both the IWW and the first Rotary club were established in Chicago in 1905.

"But don't you think there's this, Nora. Conditions as they are, don't you believe that if one is to be known and accepted as a potential force, that at the start certain superficial concessions must be made. People are deathly afraid of having to do with someone whom they suspect is out of his time, who questions, who hesitates to conform . . ."

"Yes, yes," cried Nora lifting herself on her elbow. "Yes. But people start making first concessions and it doesn't stop there!" She lay back with her cigaret, crying: "Ah, if I could go on with this truth as I know it! Take Gandhi. How they cried out on him for building great fires of the clothing English charities had sent down to his people. Ah, just there, they said, just there he could have compromised. Non-cooperation, yes, if he will, but common-sense, rational thinking. His people needed these clothes, why burn them? Ah, *there* it is!" Nora's hand closed out thin, her voice sharp with emotion. "There it is. He couldn't, he *couldn't* make that or any other concession to the forces to which he was opposed. Not even to clothe the starved sick bodies of his people—no. Clothes they needed, but what he gave them, what they stood out for, they needed more. We'll go naked if we must, he could say to them, but we can't abandon the truth of our spirit."*

Rebekah sat, vaguely nodding.

"Yes, I believe that," she said slowly. "All that is true."

---

* Following the 1919 massacre of hundreds of Indians at Amritsar by British troops, the Indian nationalist leader Mohandas Gandhi (1869–1948) led a movement of noncooperation against British rule. Sanctioned by the Indian National Congress in 1920, it focused on boycotts, resignation of titles, and refusal to pay taxes. Gandhi was arrested for sedition in 1922 and sentenced to six years in prison, but was released in February 1924.

16 Her relation with Soupault was not in her mind, never discussed nor really wondered over in her mind. She didn't want any analysis of this. Soupault was strange to her, and alone, unrelated to the mind, and so apart from any human problem. She had known him long now, but she knew that she had come just so far into him, into the knowing of his identity, his detached response to people, his hands moving agilely over sticks as he built the fires for their outdoor eatings, as though he were more drawn in these things that he touched and made serve him than in the life of any person.

She had come just so far in him, and she would never know any more of him. She knew this. And she knew that he had come in her to the same last edge of human knowing. Beyond this was the chaos of their own beings, the mystery that must remain inviolable and unarticulated. In this way they would go far from each other with other people, almost irretrievably, and then they would come back ungiven again to the strange unknown other. And Soupault was never curious about the silent stretches in her. And he was never happy, but content and incurious with her, or in fierce mad rages of joy, or cool and remote like a gold-bellied serpent, with his evil beautiful mask.

He came in upon them one evening after more than a week's silence. Kerith had lit candles below the eight-armed Buddha, and the gilded doors hung open. She wore a sea Chinese robe and red kid sandals, stirring incense at the altar. Her hands fell through smoke, bowing a slow dance through cool flowing smoke. The Pekinese bulged candle light below their brows, their eyes moved full and dark upon her, their paws sprayed yellow silk.

Soupault came from shadow and crouched, putting forward from his fingers a fine white ring. It hung frail at the turned sensitive feet of the Buddha and the full lids of Buddha accepted it. Soupault stood back in the contracting darkness, and Kerith stooped amazed and lifted the white ring.

"It is very beautiful," she said, wondering.

His body was closed silent and immune to her.

"It is for all of us," he said touching Nora's hand. His voice curved softly and tenderly about them. "It is for all three of us."

Nora held his hand with her quick uneasy fingers. She reached quickly up to him, pressing his mouth. He had turned awkward, in his timidity, watching them.

From the street door Rebekah came suddenly in to them.

"How lovely you all are!"

Nora swayed with her unspent emotion.

"We are suspended. Out of time. Out of sensation. We appear to move but we do not. We are static."

Rebekah laughed to them, holding out her hands.

"Suspend me!"

The candles shriveled into darkness and the four went, talking, into the wider room. Kerith played a cello-record of a Bach Fugue, and then a Chinese disc, high and grievous. The Pekinese awoke whimpering, Nee Nee's dark face puckered in grief, her cry tearing like thin silk in her throat. Nora lifted her quickly.

"Come, my Nee Nee child."

Nee Nee watched the sound over her light gold shoulder.

Kerith played a dance of Russian ecstatic gloom, drawing the music sharp in her arms, thrusting it from her wrists. Nora talked with Rebekah in elation. Women pickets were on hunger strike in Washington jails.

"It is our protest, our protest."

Kerith played the death song of Madame Butterfly. The high frail voice tottered in the room. In the long convulsive end, the old man appeared quietly at the door, one hand lifted below his averted face.

"May I ask you, may I ask you not to let that song continue?"

He stood old, facing them. His shoulders drooped in sorrow, his mouth fell away from his words.

"Thank you," he said quietly.

He went from them, but their eyes held him palpable between

them. Kerith's eyes moved through the hall against his closed door, against silence. Presently there were the words of H. D., disintegrate in talk, and the old man's mouth answering. But really he was with them, out of his loneliness, exchanging thoughts with them. It was against everything in his nature to be shut away from them in his little room. H. D. was an irritant to him, but the only one now upon whom he could force his will.

"Ask them to come out for coffee," said Nora eagerly to Kerith. "Yes, do ask them to come out."

They came later from the hall, the old man bowing forward to Rebekah, to Soupault. H. D. twitched at the door, smiling. When he had taken his coffee, he slipped away from them again into the office. But the old man was imminent, sitting between them, and overcome with his wish to be at one with them.

"I shall be interested in hearing of your initiation to the judicature."

He told them of his first case, examining his small fine fingernails, talking slowly, divertingly. He smiled at Rebekah.

"I shall be interested to hear. Your experience will differ from mine to just the extent that the debut of an ill-at-ease and gauche youth must differ from that of a poised and charming woman."

Rebekah laughed, bowing to him as she sat.

"But you will come, won't you?" she cried. "You'd be infinitely more satisfactory than Nora." She turned laughing to Nora. "I'm sure you wouldn't translate me into abstract terms and judge me accordingly."

"That is a compliment," said the old man graciously, "which Nora pays us all."

"Well, what are you going to do about the pickets?" said Soupault to Rebekah. It was a break to them. He felt this but his voice went on blindly. "They have a case, haven't they?"

"Yes," said Rebekah, hesitant upon the old man. And then her voice sounded firmly forward. "Yes, of course, they have a case. Don't you agree with me, Mr. Day?"

The old man leaned to drop his cigaret ash in the copper bowl.

"On the surface of the thing I can't say, Mrs. Woolf. I have not studied the points, the accusation, the finer details."

They talked on, but now the communion had lapsed from them,

and after eating, the old man bowed goodnight. And Soupault had become restless, and impatient, feeling their talk and their voices excluding him. The two women were creating a heavy subtle atmosphere of centralized and perfected accord.

Rebekah stretched in her chair, arms lifted bare and beautiful back from the fall of her sleeves. Nora leaned on the chair back, smoking, and Rebekah's hands stretched backward, falling in deep full caress upon Nora's throat. Rebekah looked fully back over her brows.

"Nora."

Nora was submerged in fore-knowing, fulfilled in the deep soft caress of Rebekah's hands.

"Nora, shall we go, shall we go on to Washington—shall we give them our protest too?"

Nora leaned, half-smiling. Rebekah's hands caressed her, fully, deeply.

"I think we should do that," Rebekah murmured full in her throat. "Go on together to Washington."

Nora leaned exhausted, as though she had begotten Rebekah.

"But you see, I can't. You know I haven't a cent. It's the thing I want most, Rebekah, it's the thing I want. But I can't do it, you know that."

Rebekah lay smiling.

"But *with* me. I'm offering it. That is what I want to do. We'll simply go on and report as pickets, and if they take us to jail, we'll do that. We'll just go on and be ready for whatever will come to us."

They swung together, purposeful, rejoicing.

"Yes," cried Nora softly. "Yes. We will do that. We must go."

17 Tarney dictated. Turned his eyes.

"Had you known that the little factory girl, little Mary, died?"

"Ah, no."

Tarney smoked. He lived.

"I tried to establish contact with her." His soft firm wrist curled in his cuff. "You were here, I believe, the day she refused to meet my mind on the matter of keeping out in the open air. It seems she had an affection of the lungs. She'd go home and sleep in a closed room. There was ignorance to combat with."

Clear light was a miracle on his flesh. His fresh lids lifted light. He breathed.

"I suggest that you take up a little collection among the office and factory workers towards purchasing a floral offering. I'll make up whatever difference there may be short of eight or ten dollars. At noon you can pick out an appropriate piece."

He stirred.

"Poor girl."

Kerith typed the morning at her desk, outraged. She was too busy to know. Only the circle in which they moved protected, rejected him. She would never go out among those people asking for money for Mary's wreath. Never. She saw the right of Tarney's indurate being, and the perfect fulfillment of his life. He came to her desk.

"Will you get hold of the Business Men's Club and order lunch. Served about one-thirty. Get the chef on the phone. Tell him Tarney, of course, and three guests. Four squabs. That would be nice, eh? Four squabs. What would you suggest, Miss Day? French fries and asparagus? How does that sound? Salad with thousand island dressing?"

Kerith at the phone felt resolve forming in her. The voice of the chef, subservient.

"Would Mr. Tarney finish with Baked Alaska and coffee?"

Tarney full at her elbow, watering.

"Baked Alaska, Mr. Tarney?"

"Yes, by all means, Baked Alaska."

Kerith walked into his office. This was *done.* He startled in his chair.

"Is there any trouble? Can I offer you a more interesting compensation for your work?"

In every part of her purpose strode.

"No."

"But what is it then? Are you ill?"

"No, I feel that I must go. That is all."

It was simple and absolute to talk with him so, and they were more at ease with each other than ever before. He protested, but his eyes were unencroaching, accepting her.

"But not at once. We can discuss this."

Her voice swept under the sudden wave of elation. There was no necessity of assertion, no oppression of being. She could go easily and simply on, without assertion or responsibility. Her eyes reached beyond to the red flag of sun against the window.

"Yes, at once," she said, almost smiling to him. In her heart she knew it was the end of false work. She would never work again for conditions as they were.

She went down into the bleak narrow street, into the feel of snow. Car rails stretched tight, buildings gnawing the crisp white leaf of the sky. Her blood throbbed to the final freedom, but her mind was cool. Her mind moved cool over the buildings, acknowledging their puissance. She knew that the being of subjugation was still vital. Her mind knew the illusion of escape, but her blood beat up in denial.

She rode in the streetcar seeing the faces, glutted faces, bodies glossed in afflux, and bodies sucked flat, eyes quenched. She rode to Mount Auburn, walked the thin street, climbed stairs to Soupault's empty room. She waited alone in his chair by the gas fire.

Presently it began to snow, soft full white mouths pressing the window. Kerith watched the stalks of the trees turn soft, the brick wall clinging soft to the ground, the street falling away. The soft white emotion of snow diffusing the sharp stalks beyond the window, and she was closed away, with the hard chairs and straight-limbed bed striking clear.

She pressed the cold flesh of her palms against her cheeks, and the cold hard flesh was like a miracle on her face. She opened her hands at the fire and looked down into the webbed dark lines that twisted in her palms. Her hands were long and hard before her like miraculous instruments.

"I am the miracle," she said looking into her hands, "I am the perfect ego released."

She lay back, calming her mind out of her, willing it away from her body. She began slowly to think of people, isolating them. Women who were freed through political consciousness, still charming. Charming intelligent people. Mrs. Speyer exclaiming: "Why can't people cry 'Tender Buttons' to each other instead of 'Good morning!'"* Why indeed? Perfect charming intelligent civilization, or foul unjust development of the resources of man. It all depended on which side you turn the cloth.

"If I don't believe in my own experience," said Kerith, "I am lost."

Soupault walked into the fire-darkness. His books patterned on the bed.

"Halloo."

He leaned above her, and her blood ran suddenly dark and warm.

"How long have you been here?" he said. His breath was cold and sharp over her hair.

"All afternoon."

He wondered. "Impossible."

"I've given it up," she said.

"Why?"

Freedom beat suddenly rich under the destitution of words. Soupault leaned.

---

* This is a reference to Gertrude Stein's innovative and amusing *Tender Buttons: Objects, Food, Rooms* (1914).

"It possessed me. I wanted to set that part of life definitely away. I'll never again work for those conditions."

He crouched at the logs, stretching out his thin hands to the warmth. His neck leaned gold-edged on darkness.

"I won't take any more part in it," she said.

Soupault spoke into flame, voice clear.

"My show is meaningless too. My graduation. It can't mean anything."

Soupault swayed on his thighs, face lifted, half in light.

"What will you do?"

Kerith laughed.

"I have no money."

Soupault watched the flame, and spoke: "I have a little saved."

He talked into flame.

"I have thought of things to be done," he said. "France. In Brittany. I have known places. There are things one could do. One could simply go away. Something is possible. I don't know."

She saw his fine high face against flame, the hard brow, and the full heavy hair curved above his ear into his neck. Her mind was darkness, her eyes on his light gold face against flame. She sat still.

"But you can't go now," she said. "The university. The army."

He crouched at the fire, fingers like narrow sticks across it.

"If I cannot stay," he said quietly.

He sat up, laughing, his quick wolfish smile catching the flame.

"I can't take life so seriously," he said.

"I know," said Kerith, knowing so deeply that this was true. "There is no necessity."

"We'll just go away together," said Soupault.

"Until the time comes to go on to something else," she said.

They were in a time of suspension now, busy with their plans for getting away. She staid apart from Nora with this, in fear of breaking the miraculous moment. She moved with Soupault, sure above the undercurrent of negation. Nora was apart from them, and dooming, like the inevitable return to the acceptance of caring, of self-demolition.

She felt that now that there was decision in herself she could establish final relationships, of coming together with H. D. in a passion of alliance. She wanted to help him over the accounts as he worked in the dark office, but she could never reach the words to offer him this.

When Soupault was in school, for they would wait until the end of the month and his army pay, she was alone, reading, or walking in the snow that had fallen at intervals for several days.

She walked in the snow, detached from her actual movement in life, and in strange delight. She lifted her chin, feeling the arrogant thrust of her face against snow.

Men slipped past her on the snow, awkward with cold. She was in the university grounds, walking along the woods, water crisp on the lake with steel light of the sun like a stiff fallen shield. She went down the curve, the flakes disintegrate before her, breaking over the loom of a figure walking in the sheer dripping snow. The dark bulk of Brodsky progressed before her, and she ran after him in a flurry of delight, putting her arm through his arm, close to him.

They walked, following the trunks of trees they knew, for the paths were covered and the road gone under the fragile drifts of snow. Kerith ran ahead from him crying: "Do you remember this tree, Brodsky? Do you remember this one?"

Brodsky came, nodding his head down, touching the wet bark. They knew these, walking at night under the stars. From one bush they had whittled boughs, and they found the broken stab of the branches, flesh of their hands sharp crimson against snow. Brodsky slipped heavily as they walked, and lifted himself laughing and shaking away the heavy clots of snow.

"We are living wholly on our reputations," he said laughing. "I have grown too aged even to walk."

Kerith stirred then to tell him of Soupault, but this union was too untouched. She thought: "Later I will say it. That we are going away."

She danced hard quick little steps over the snow.

"Do you *remember*," hammered Brodsky, filled with the awareness of their union, and their content. "'The pure products of America go crazy.'"*

"It has been approaching all my life," cried Kerith. "And it is here. It is at last here!"

Brodsky was heavy with their oneness, smiling secretly down his flat white cheeks.

---

* These are the opening lines of William Carlos Williams's "To Elsie" from *Spring and All* (1923).

"Delicious madness," he said. "I have cast much from me. Soul-seriousness I have cast from me. I am beginning to sense how beautiful the pattern of my life can be. I have broken myself up, creating of myself malleable material. The recombinations, the possible arrangements entice me."

He watched the flakes that gathered softly on the back of his glove, melting slowly to the dark damp skin of the glove. His face hung heavy, but breathless and eager over the flakes. He looked up to her quickly, with quick winsome charm: "They're lovely, aren't they?"

Kerith drew his hand up quickly against her mouth.

"Brodsky, my heart is filled with love for you."

They walked on, her fingers dropped sensitive on the bare flesh of his wrist.

"It is true," she said presently, "we love each other."

He covered her hand. They walked quietly together.

"Love," he said finally, tasting the word. He lifted his shoulders, smiling. "It seems a little past the time, doesn't it? It seems to me the emotional response you want is dead."

Kerith's blood went cool in her veins. Her voice struck dull.

"Response to what?"

He set his profile against her.

"I am not a fool," he said, "I am not a fool."

She saw that he was limping now.

"I'm afraid that you are getting cold," she said. She was incurious for his voice, his death complete in her blood. The icy burden of his death spread in her.

They walked into the streets, soundless into the road to town. His silence loomed ahead to the break of his voice. She walked, knowing it would come, suspended in the dread of his voice. They came down past the factories that hedged the shop, and above the last long slope Brodsky cleared his throat.

"I don't know what you wanted of *me*," he said. "I've not been blind to all that has happened. I've known in a degree what was going on."

Kerith walked cold beside him. His voice was the impeccable word of loathing. She walked cold with revulsion and rage.

"It must be with you—will to power," he said. "I can't go beyond that."

"It was not that," said Kerith.

"It's the only explanation," he said. "The will to subject me too."

Kerith felt for words.

"You don't understand. Is it because of my identity with another person that you withdraw from me? I have wanted a separate relation with you. I have always wanted this. You have acknowledged the essential me, you have believed in the creation of life within life. In this we have known each other. But this cannot immune me from relations beyond you, which do not concern you, but me and another person."

"What did you really want of me?" repeated Brodsky.

Kerith spread her hands.

"What have I wanted of Nora, of Soupault? It has to progress alone. I can't know."

The spoken names struck flame in his face. He turned to her, hostile head swinging heavy with malignant strength. Kerith saw him transfigured in his hate.

"Well, I won't serve your purpose as they do!" His voice swung strongly upon her. "That's what amazes you, isn't it? If you can't break me into your mold, you don't want me. Very well. I won't change. I won't be shouted into your inquisitorial freedom. It's without pride, without dignity." He lifted his head, flaming down upon her, and she stood looking at him and wondering how much of truth there was in what he was saying. "What is it you fling at us," he cried to her, "'you who are not with me, oppose me!'"*

Kerith nodded.

"Yes, that's it."

"And a noble lofty cry it is!" he exclaimed in bitter disgust.

"I am not noble, I am not lofty," explained Kerith. "That is why you resent me."

The bowling menacing voice lighted depths of laughter in her. She turned walking from it and down to the shop. Rebekah's car stood at the kerb, lights dimmed. Brodsky went to it.

---

* In Matt. 12:30 Jesus says: "He who is not with me is against me, and he who does not gather with me scatters."

"You won't come in with me?" said Kerith at the door.

He leaned, opening the car door under the gathering snow.

"Rebekah will be going along soon. I'll wait."

He hunched in the back seat, malignant in the dark, arms crossed.

Kerith came from him into the living room and to the kitchen beyond. Nora had begun dinner at the range and Rebekah leaned near the door, talking, pulling on her gloves slowly.

"You have a most charming escort awaiting you in the car," said Kerith.

Rebekah smiled, raising her dark full brows.

"Good," she said. "If the starter is frozen he can crank."

"I shouldn't count on it," said Kerith. "I feel quite sure he won't."

Rebekah was lazy and poised, smiling.

"And why *won't* he?"

She laughed at Kerith and pulled up suddenly, moving to the door.

"I love it to be cold," she said, fastening up her high collar. Then she turned back to them. "By the way," she said, "it just occurred to us last night that the Company's Convention is being held in Washington this month."

There was a slow ominous pause. Nora worked at the range, her lids fallen.

"Max was amused at the thought of me speaking all fall in the interests of the company, *as* a Republican, and the flying in their faces at the convention."

Nora looked up to her fully, unshaken.

"But you mustn't feel that you are pledged to me. I know it's important for Max that you keep in their good graces."

"But of course we're going on!" cried Rebekah. "I hadn't thought of that. I hadn't thought for a minute of giving up the trip." She drew at her gloves. "There'll be just this difference. I'll have to be in evidence at the convention. We'll go on just as we planned, and you can go ahead in every way that turns up, but I'll have to take a less active part in it."

Nora stood away, unbroken eyes in Rebekah.

"Oh, no."

She smiled against her emotion, talking lightly.

"No, if it's so I can't accept my part of it. I just don't want to go in that way, that's all."

Rebekah laughed.

"Isn't that rather ridiculous, Nora?"

"No. Not if I feel so. I do not question your decision in the matter. It is splendid that we both know so clearly for ourselves."

"Ah, well . . ."

Rebekah pulled at her gloves, facing Nora. She smiled.

"Nora, you can't go on this way, simply creating scruples. What will it lead to? What do you ever expect to do? It's impossible."

"I may never do anything," said Nora. Her voice trembled in her mouth. "But you have really no right to that. That is a part of me. I admire you because you know so clearly what you must do, what you want. But what I feel is surely a part of me. And as for starting out now on a crusade of protest with you, why I couldn't, I just couldn't. I know my north star too. When I say I could not, you must understand that it is so."

Rebekah drew closed in herself. Kerith saw the sharp bridle of her body, and then her head turned quickly to Kerith as Nora bent over the stove. Rebekah's eyes on Kerith were wide with the distress of this, and dark with a subtle terrible pity. Kerith knew that if she accepted this look it would be the final betrayal of Nora, the absolute denial of her. She stood cold and quiet, staring cool and uncommitted into Rebekah's eyes.

"I'm sorry," said Rebekah, and she went to the door.

18 Sunday H. D. cut oranges in quarters, sucked them with the skin pressed flat in his lips. Shadows on the glass-topped table curled green under the plates. Kerith poured water for her tea, lingering above the blue flame that sprang against the sauce pan. She turned to the suck of fruit, dropping her hand at the table edge.

"You didn't see what Soupault gave me."

It was a torture to her to speak to him after the months of silence across the table. H. D. looked up to her face, startled, a square of orange pressed on his teeth. Kerith turned her hand at the table edge.

"Here."

He looked down and blood mounted his skin, mounted to his seeing eyes. The ring was white and hard on her finger.

"Well!"

He dried his fingertips and with the long nail of his last finger lifted a bit of pulp from between his teeth. It was bitter for him too to speak with her, and he stood up with a queer unsteadiness, clinging to the silence between them.

"Well, what's that mean?"

His mouth drew tight against its tremulous movement. He lifted his hand unsteadily to her shoulder, patting her gently. His lips fumbled.

"We are going to France," said Kerith. She was grateful for the silent white ring whose presence he could understand.

He stood trembling before her, and Kerith put her arms about him, and the dreadful given release of his body broke against her. She felt herself enormous and puissante above him, holding him against her, but her mind was threshing in dark confusion. Their emotions were pressing to go down in a perfect tide of atonement, but their bodies enclosed them, static in opposition. There was no relief from the extraneous fact of their living, no liberation from the touch of the other. She held him close, knowing the hard bone of his brow against her breasts.

They heard the street door open, saw sun fall solid in the dark hall. Soupault walked, peering into the gloom. H. D. hung away, flushed and sheepish, fingertips twitching at his sides. Kerith left them together and came to Nora. They listened to the hesitant voices of the two men in the library, H. D. questioning and unsure and Soupault's slow strange response.

Kerith talked with Nora but she could almost not bear to really see her, the unreproachful face, Nora's profound response to the thrill of Kerith's going. It was in their souls as the logical progress but Kerith could think only that now Nora would be alone, that there would be no one. Kerith couldn't believe that the spiritual acquiescence in this could finally matter. No matter what Nora spiritually wanted, her body must stay in the shop alone. But she knew she couldn't go back, even if it killed Nora. The experience was through for her, and there could be no reiteration. And Nora was like a wound in her.

They walked out together, the four, up Eden Park where the snow was broken apart in new green wounds. Nora walked fresh and slender with H. D., in a quiver of response to the solid dark snow-clouds, and the trees mottling the slopes, the water stretched taut between banks. Their footsteps were caught frozen in the brittle white path by the bush.

H. D. smiled quickly as he talked with them, his throat swallowed. Nora called out to them at a shatter of snow birds in the path. H. D. quickened, coming up to her. His soles were thin, slipping in the sharp path. Kerith felt them the four of them dark slow points moving in an infinite world. The white sluggish world lay inert, unaroused, and they moved forward without skill, infinitesimal points in the sluggish flow.

In his mind H. D. was turning from them, turning back to the shop, going over the ledgers, being possessed again by the life of the shop. He stood tapping at the snow with one foot, drifting his hands in the pockets of his overcoat.

"Well, I'll guess I'll be getting back to the shop."

Nora took his arm, drawing him on with them.

"NO, no. Today you must stay. You must stay with me."

He shrank back from them all, smiling.

"No, I'll have to go back."

He stood looking out over the closed waters. He was will-less, wanting adequate subjection. There was no portentous subtle force in them willing him on, and the habit of his life was sucking him away. He would get back to the shop, he would get back to the old man. He smiled, slipping away over the path.

Under the glass-brittle sheets of light they went down from him, sliding apart from their held hands, crying to each other with laughter. The music rotunda stood isolate like a betrayed thing, reproachful, stroking blue shadows on the snow. They followed each other, running with snow-slowed steps on the low curved wall. The trees were weighted low in the cold, clinging to their snow, the bone-boughs hard and unbroken under the crisp white flesh.

KAY BOYLE (1902–92) was one of the most resilient of the American artists who lived in Paris in the 1920s. She published more than forty books, including novels, short fiction, poetry, children's books, memoirs, and translations. Her work has appeared in magazines ranging from *This Quarter* and *transition* to the *New Yorker,* the *Saturday Evening Post,* and *The Nation.* She received two O. Henry Awards for Best Short Story of the Year, two Guggenheim Fellowships, honorary degrees, membership in the American Academy of Arts and Letters, and a Senior Fellowship from the National Endowment for the Arts.

SANDRA SPANIER is an associate professor of English at Pennsylvania State University. She is the author of *Kay Boyle: Artist and Activist.* She is the editor of *Life Being the Best and Other Stories* by Kay Boyle and *Love Goes to Press,* a previously unpublished 1946 play by Martha Gellhorn and Virginia Cowles, and the coeditor of *American Fiction, American Myth: Essays by Philip Young.*

Composed in 10.5/14 Filosophia
with Futura display
by Celia Shapland
for the University of Illinois Press
Designed by Cope Cumpston
Manufactured by Thomson-Shore, Inc.

University of Illinois Press
1325 South Oak Street
Champaign, IL 61820-6903
www.press.uillinois.edu